Thor needs to find someone who can grant Isaac, his best friend's boyfriend and a human, immortality. It's not something he's had to worry about before, but he wants to do this for Tryg.

Cecil is running from his brother. He's been running for decades, and he's relieved to have an opportunity to stop for a while when Thor contacts him. He meets Thor and his friends in Brussels — and so does Fabrice, his brother.

Cecil is used to being on the run, but he's usually alone.

Not anymore.

He's made Isaac immortal, and Thor and Tryg want to thank him by helping him to get rid of his brother. Fabrice is powerful, though, and none of them know exactly how much, not even Cecil.

But they're going to find out.

Like Storms
Copyright © 2019 Catherine Lievens
ISBN: 978-1-4874-2680-4
Cover art by Angela Waters

Published by eXtasy Books Inc or
Devine Destinies, an imprint of eXtasy Books Inc

Look for us online at:
www.eXtasybooks.com or www.devinedestinies.com

LIKE STORMS
VIKINGS BOOK 2

BY

CATHERINE LIEVENS

CHAPTER ONE

His job was getting old — and fast. Thorvald supposed it had been a while coming, though. He'd been the handler for a small team of professional assassins for the past fifty or so years, if memory served him right. Maybe Tryg had the right idea thinking about retiring. Of course, he was thinking about doing that because he'd met Isaac, not because he'd had enough of making sure the bad people in the world got what they deserved. Tryg might have said he wasn't retiring, just pulling back slightly, but Thor wasn't an idiot. What were the odds that Tryg would be ready to travel hundreds of miles for a job when Isaac was at home waiting for him? Especially with how they'd met and found each other.

Isaac was strong, but that didn't change the fact that he'd been kidnapped and abused or that someone had tried to have him killed — and that *he* had killed that man. He needed Tryg, and not just because Tryg knew a lot of supernatural people and they were trying to make Isaac as immortal as Tryg and Thor were.

Thor's phone pinged. He was glad to stop trying to match up assassins to jobs for a while. Tryg was one of the few who'd ever said no — he didn't kill people who didn't deserve it, and in the past few years, Thor had stopped accepting the jobs Tryg would have refused anyway. But some people still tried to convince him to take them, and making that decision always meant a lot of research and poking around in things Thor didn't want to touch with a ten-foot pole.

Skype? the text read.

Thor put the phone down and opened the app on his computer. His smile widened when Tryg answered. "Weren't you on vacation?"

"Shut it," Tryg grumbled.

Thor laughed. He couldn't help it. Tryg had wanted to take Isaac to the beach for the first time in Isaac's life, and he'd done it, which explained why his usually pale skin was bright pink and freckled. "There's a reason we avoid the sun, you know?"

"I do now."

"You should have used sunscreen."

"I did. Wasn't enough."

"It's going to hurt."

"Already does. Are you done?"

Thor laughed again and leaned back in his chair. "Sure. Actually, wait." He leaned forward again and pressed a few keys. "There. I got a screenshot."

Tryg flipped him the bird. "You're an asshole."

"I know, but you love me anyway. How's Isaac?"

The scowl faded from Tryg's face, and it was as if it had never been there. "He's doing great. He still has nightmares, but I expected that. We're dealing as well as we can, which is fucking good, considering everything. But then, he's strong. He's shown that more than once."

"He still doesn't want you to retire?"

"He says he doesn't. He wants me to hunt the monsters, and I kind of want to, you know? I want to protect the Isaacs of this world, but I also don't want to let him out of my sight. No matter how strong he is, he's been through hell and back, and that will take time to fade. I don't want to be in Africa or whatever when he wakes up from a nightmare. Besides, I have to focus on finding someone who can make him immortal. I'm not about to lose him, even if it's to old age."

"Right." Thor knew Tryg had been worried about that.

He'd never been one to relax, and he'd lost too many people to be able to let this go. He would not rest until he was sure Isaac wasn't going anywhere, whatever that entailed. "I've been doing some research."

Tryg leaned forward. "What did you find?"

"There's talk about mages, witches, that kind of thing."

"With all the creatures out there, there's bound to be someone who can do this, right?"

"If there is, I'll find them. I promise." Be it the last thing Thor did. He'd never thought either of them would find this kind of happiness, and he would make sure Tryg could keep it.

They weren't friends. They weren't brothers. They were something more, something there was no word for because they'd known each other for eight hundred years, and they'd been close every single second of those years.

"I should help you find this person," Tryg said.

"No, you shouldn't. I'm better than you with research and computers, and you need to spend time with Isaac. I don't have anyone waiting for me to come home from work. You do. Besides, you're retired, yeah?"

Tryg chuckled. "Not yet, although I doubt I'll be accepting jobs anytime soon. Even if you find someone who can help, Isaac and I will probably have to travel, and like you said, I want to focus on him."

"Coming to New York?"

"Maybe. We're going to get used to seeing each other often if I do, though."

"I don't see how that could be a bad thing." Tryg was the only person close to family Thor had, and it was tempting to tell him he wanted to go with him and Isaac when they went looking for the mage.

And why not? It wasn't like Thor needed to work. He'd been working for hundreds of years. He had enough money saved and enough investments to live for another eight hundred years without working a day. It would be boring, so he couldn't do that, but he could take a decade or two off and help Tryg and Isaac.

That was — if they wanted him around. It was probably a moot point to ask now, since they had no idea where to start, but Thor wanted to be sure before he started making plans.

He cleared his throat. "You'll need help once I find you a mage."

"We will? I'm pretty sure I can convince anyone to help, if I put my mind to it."

Thor snorted. "Isaac would probably be more successful."

"Just come out with it, Thor. I don't have all day." Tryg glanced to the side, and Thor suspected he knew what Tryg was seeing. Isaac was waiting for Tryg, maybe asleep, maybe reading. Whatever Isaac was doing, though, Tryg wanted to get back to him, and he would as soon as this call was over.

The thought made Thor's heart squeeze. He wanted what Tryg and Isaac had, but he didn't resent Tryg for finding it while he hadn't. He was immortal. He had plenty of time to find someone who would tolerate his presence for the rest of their lives.

"I'd like to come with you," he said.

Tryg blinked. "To talk to the mage?"

"Yes."

"You know you don't have to come."

"I *want* to. I want to spend more time with you and get to know Isaac. It's about time, yeah?"

Thor hadn't thought Tryg's smile could get wider, but it did. "It is. Let me know when you find someone, and Isaac and I will start planning our trip to New York. Unless you want to meet somewhere else?"

"Let me do a little research before you get on a plane. It won't be much use if the mage is close to where you are right now."

"I'm not going to say no to more vacation, although I wish it wasn't on the beach," Tryg grumbled.

"You were the one who took Isaac to the beach."

"I didn't think I'd hate it so much."

"Yet you'll do it again if that's what he wants."

Tryg's expression softened. "Yeah, I would. Isaac deserves to have anything he wants."

And that was what Thor wanted to find — someone for whom he'd be happy to do things he hated.

Cecil gently squeezed the melon and raised it to his nose. It smelled ripe, so he put it in his bag. He still needed bread, and maybe one of those tiny cakes he was so fond of.

God, he loved living in Paris. He wished he didn't have to leave soon. He couldn't stay in one place too long, not if he wanted to make sure his brother wouldn't find him, but he'd leave a piece of his heart in Paris, dammit. He hated when this happened. He should have realized it would, though. He loved Europe, especially the north.

On a whim, he grabbed a bouquet of colorful flowers and headed to the bread department. He also loved grocery shopping in Paris, with the breads and chocolates, although he'd gained a bit of weight because of that — and because he didn't enjoy any kind of sport or physical activity. It wasn't like anyone complained, though. Cecil supposed that was one perk of living alone and hiding for most of his life.

His phone rang just as he walked into his apartment. He rushed his bags to the kitchen, both of them toppling over when he put them onto the counter to get his phone out of his pocket. He grinned when he saw the name on the screen and caught the melon before it could roll to the floor. "Mabel!" He hadn't heard from her in too long. It was unavoidable, but still. Her absence in his life made it even lonelier than it usually was.

"I didn't interrupt anything, did I?" Mabel asked.

"Of course not. You know that."

She huffed. "Being in hiding doesn't mean you can't find someone to fuck, Cecil. You have needs."

"Not really." He'd been without sex for so long that he didn't feel the need for it anymore. His hand and the few toys he'd collected were more than enough, and he didn't have to fear them talking to the wrong people. That had happened a few times, and he wasn't ready to repeat that mistake.

"Whatever. What are you up to if not seducing the cute Frenchies?"

"Not much. Grocery shopping. I've been writing new spells."

"Why do you even do that?"

"Because it's a way to pass the time. I can't spend my days watching TV." And he liked to think of new ways to do things. He might not need to say spells out loud like the witches in the movies, but writing them down helped him think of the magic he could use and how to use it. It was finicky, and Cecil was proud to say he was one of the best in his field—probably because he was one of the few who had the time to do it. He didn't have a lot of clients, since they might lead Fabrice to him, and that was the one thing that couldn't happen, not since Cecil liked his limbs where they were—attached to his body.

"Anyway, I called because I might have found you a job."

Cecil opened the fridge with his free hand and deposited the melon onto one of the shelves. "You know I'm not taking clients right now." He would have to do that soon, though, because he enjoyed living like he was. He couldn't leave his apartment often, and he couldn't spend time with people, but he could read and watch movies, and that meant he was using up the money he'd saved from the last jobs he'd done.

"You'll want to take this one."

"Why?"

"Well, it's a guy who wants to be immortal."

Cecil faked a yawn. "Boring. Everyone wants to be immortal."

"You're probably right, but it's not the guy per se who's interesting. The one who called is."

"Why?"

"Because I poked around when I heard he was looking for immortality, and I discovered he's a draugr."

That got Cecil's attention. He was immortal, yet since he'd spent most of his life in his apartment, he'd never met a draugr. They were rare, since they were created through a series of events that didn't happen often, and nowadays, only a few were born every decade. "A draugr?"

"Yes. I haven't contacted him, since I didn't want to draw his attention, but I gave that email of yours to the person he talked to. He probably already wrote to you."

For once, Cecil couldn't wait to turn his computer on. "Do you have any more details?"

"Nope. The only reason I have what I have is that I dug a bit, but like I said, I didn't want the guy to realize I was looking into him. He's a loner like you, but from what I understand, he coordinates a group of supernatural assassins."

Cecil's stomach dropped. That didn't sound good, or like a man he wanted to help. "Assassins?" His brother was a killer. It wasn't the same thing, he supposed, but it was too similar for his peace of mind.

"Only bad people, from what I know, and the guy doesn't do any killing himself. I know you don't like this, but he's ready to pay well, and I know you need the money. Maybe talk to him and decide after you have more details? You *need* this job, hon. We both know that."

Cecil did, and the fact that the guy was a draugr was only one reason for him to accept. "I'll check in with him." He had to.

And he wanted to.

He'd never been good at resisting temptations — which was why his waist was thicker than it ought to be — so as soon as he and Mabel hung up, he opened his computer, logging in as he finished putting away the groceries. Sure enough, there was an email waiting for him in between the spam and time-limited offers.

Cecil tried to steady his churning stomach and clicked open the email.

The guy was looking for a mage who could make someone immortal. There weren't a lot of them, but Cecil was part of that small group. The guy — Thorvald — had written a few details in the email, but not nearly as many as Cecil needed or wanted. It was obvious the job wasn't for Thorvald, though, since he was a draugr. Probably for someone Thorvald loved, though. If he'd met a nice human girl and wanted to keep her in his life, he'd need to find a way, and Cecil hoped his way wasn't to hire the first mage he could find to make her immortal. Some mages only cared about money, and they wouldn't care if Thorvald and his girl had only known each other three months and would end up trying to kill each other in a year or two.

Cecil tapped his fingertips on the table. He was curious. He wanted to meet this Thorvald and find out more about him. He'd always wanted to meet a draugr. They were the magical being everyone wanted to be — it was next to impossible to kill them, as far as Cecil knew, and they could shift into various animals, and into *smoke*. He wanted to find out if there were other things they could do and if he could learn things from them that would be useful in his art as a mage.

He wasn't sure he could trust Thorvald, though, and he

wouldn't be sure until he met the guy. He could do a little research of his own, so he opened the browser and got onto the gray web.

The gray web was reserved for supernatural beings. There were a lot of them in the world, and it was a way to get in contact with other creatures like archness in Greece or kakis in Japan. Thorvald might not be on it, although from what Mabel had told Cecil, Cecil doubted that was the case. But he'd find someone who knew him.

He did. He found a chat thread that talked about supernatural assassins and which ones were the best, Thorvald and some of his co-workers were talked about as having too many morals and only accepting jobs that dealt with criminals.

That was a good thing, and it soothed Cecil's worries. It didn't mean he would say yes, but he *could* meet Thorvald and his girlfriend, or whoever he wanted to have become immortal. Then he'd decide.

Thor expected the text that made his phone ping to be from Tryg. He was the only person who texted Thor these days, although he'd gotten a tentative message from Isaac after Tryg had bought him a phone.

But this text wasn't from either of them. It was a blocked number, so Thor's hackles rose, but he checked it anyway. He needed to know who had his number and where they'd gotten it—and more importantly, *why* they'd looked for it.

Heard you were looking for a mage?

Thor frowned. He *was* looking for a mage, and he hadn't made a secret of it. Still, he didn't like this. *I am.* He stared at the three bouncing dots and waited for an answer.

You're in luck, then.

Am I?

Considering I'm a mage, yeah.

That was good, better than what Thor had expected. He

had no idea how the mage had found his number, since Thor had limited himself to emailing the guy at the address he'd been given, but he'd find out soon enough.

How did you get my number? he asked.

Did a little digging. I had to make sure you were okay to contact. You wouldn't believe how many people want to become immortal.

Thor could easily imagine that. He'd seen the worst of what people could be and do in his long life. *I don't. I already am immortal.*

Draugr, yeah. I know. It's one of the reasons I want to meet with you and your . . . friend.

Thor's lips quirked. He wasn't sure why the emphasis on the word friend, but he wanted to find out. *When and where?*

I'm in Europe right now.

We can be there tomorrow. The cost wouldn't be a problem. He, Tryg, and Isaac could be on the next flight out, although it depended on where in Europe they needed to go and whether they decided they wanted to travel together.

Give me a few days. I'll need to travel, too.

So the mage wasn't going to meet them in his home — or in her home. Thor had no idea who he was talking with, but the person was smart. They knew better than to give out their address. *No problem. Just let me know where and when, and we'll be there.*

Good. Brussels. Three days from now.

Thor blinked. Brussels felt like a random city, although that might be because he'd never been there. Maybe not choosing a busier city like Paris or London was a good thing, or maybe this mage just liked mussels. *Like I said, we'll be there,* he answered.

What do you look like?

Thor cocked his head. This wasn't going the way he'd expected. *Why do you want to know?*

So I know who to look for.

No red roses?

10

Ah, no. I bet you're blond, though.

How do you know?

Draugr, remember?

Thor barked out a laugh. He didn't know what this mage looked like, but he liked them. *I remember, trust me. And yes, I'm blond. Short hair, gray eyes, lip piercing, a few tats.*

Tall?

Yeah.

Do you look even remotely like the guy in the movie?

Thor grinned and leaned back in his office chair, propping his feet on his desk. *Why does everyone always ask that?*

Between being a draugr, blond, and being named Thor, I'm not sure why you're surprised.

True. Thor had had more than one person throwing themselves at him and asking him if he was related to that actor. *He's Australian. I'm not.*

You're from Scandinavia, yes?

Yeah. This would be easier if I could call you, you know?

It was a shot in the dark, even though it *would* be easier. But Thor wanted to hear this mage's voice. He wanted to know if he was talking to a man or a woman, and if they were as fun in person as they were over texts. He wanted to get to know the mage, because there was no way either he or Tryg were letting Isaac anywhere near this person without vetting them first. He doubted the mage would mind, since they seemed to have done the same thing.

Thor's phone rang in his hand. "My full name is Thorvald," he answered the blocked number.

"Not Thor, God of thunder?" a male voice asked.

"No, although Thorvald means follower of Thor."

"Close enough, I guess, especially if you're as tall and blond as you claim."

"You know my name, but I don't know yours," Thor rumbled. He didn't understand why he was this curious, and he didn't think the why mattered.

11

There was a pause, then the mage said, "Cecil."

It was an unusual name, but then, who was *Thorvald* to judge. "Nice to meet you, Cecil."

"I know you're not the one who wants to become immortal, so who is it? Why aren't they the ones talking with me?"

"Right to the point, I see."

"I have to be. I need to make sure I can trust you and your friend before I agree to meet."

"You already agreed to meet us."

"And I can as easily stay home and send you on a wild goose chase."

Thor *definitely* liked this guy. "I have a best friend."

"And you want him to be immortal."

Thor's smile widened. "Can I talk? Because it'll be faster if I do."

"I'm zipping my mouth shut."

"Right. As I was saying, I have a best friend. He's also a draugr, and he recently met a human he fell in love with." Thor didn't explain how Isaac and Tryg had met or what had happened. Cecil didn't need to know that.

"And he wants the human to become immortal."

Thor rolled his eyes. "He does. Isaac . . . he hasn't had an easy life, at all. He's happy with Tryg, and they both expected it would take years, possibly more, to find someone who could help with the mortality, which is why they've already started looking. I was lucky to find someone who knew some-one who gave me your email address, I guess."

"What's in this for you? I can meet with your friend and his boyfriend, no problem. I can't promise I'll say yes, because that will depend on how I feel about them, but I don't under-stand what you have to do with this, though."

Thor had expected the question. "Tryg and I have been friends for hundreds of years. I want him to be happy, and that will only happen if he has Isaac with him for as long as he can. I don't want him to have to watch another love die, not when there might be a way to avoid it. He'd do the same for me, and since research is what I do, I don't mind taking care of this while he takes care of Isaac."

Cecil hummed. "I see. You sound like a good man."

"I like to think I am."

"Even though you're the handler for a group of professional killers."

Thor wasn't surprised Cecil knew. He'd done his homework, that was for sure. "I can't say that all the people I've ever worked with are good people, but I do try to make sure they only accept jobs that are warranted. Human traffickers, drug dealers, you get the idea. Many people want them dead to take their place, or to gain something from their death, or even because it's the only way they will ever pay." He hoped Cecil understood that sometimes, human justice couldn't do anything to help with that, and that those monsters needed to pay. He didn't know where Cecil's magic came from, though, so he might be a human who hadn't seen how harsh the world and the people who inhabited it could be.

Cecil cleared his throat. "Brussels, three days from now."

Thor didn't let the change of topic surprise him. "Where and when exactly?"

"I'll text you." Cecil hung up.

Thor blinked, but he didn't have time to waste. He quickly dialed Tryg's number even as he rose from his chair and headed toward his bedroom to pack.

"Thor?" Tryg asked when he answered.

"You and Isaac need to get a move on."

"You found someone?"

"Yeah. He's agreed to meet us in Brussels in three days."

"We're coming to New York. We can travel together from there."

"I'll be waiting for you."

CHAPTER TWO

Thor threw open the door of his apartment and stared as Tryg almost fell flat on his face as he tried to get a massive suitcase out of the elevator. Tryg swore and barely managed to stay on his feet, but the suitcase seemed to be stuck. Then a tiny — for Thor anyway — man hopped from the elevator over the suitcase and unstuck it, dragging it out. Even from where he was, Thor saw Tryg's eye roll. It made him chuckle, which got Tryg's attention.

Tryg glared at Thor. "You could help, you know," he mumbled as he took the suitcase from Isaac's hands and rolled it to Thor's door.

"I could have, but watching you struggle was too entertaining."

Tryg punched Thor's shoulder, then reached for him and pulled him into a hug. Thor wrapped his arms around him and squeezed, briefly closing his eyes because it felt like coming home.

He and Tryg hadn't known each other when they'd become draugr. They'd met hundreds of years after that, but they'd still been friends for close to eight hundred years, and that made Tryg more than family. "It's been too long," Thor murmured.

"Damn right. Why is it that I have to be in danger of dying or needing life or death help for you to move your ass and meet me?"

Thor laughed as he leaned back. "What can I say? I'm lazy."

Tryg punched Thor again. "Which is also why you work behind the scenes."

"Well, yeah. Doesn't mean I don't know what I'm doing, though, and I haven't seen you rejecting my research."

"Only because you know what you're doing." Tryg grabbed the suitcase and pushed its handle into Thor's hands. "You can take that to the guest room."

Thor eyed it. "You know it's too big for us to travel with it to Brussels, right?"

"I know. We're going to open it and grab what we need, then leave the rest here."

Thor had to chuckle at that. "You're using my guest room as a closet?" He rolled the thing inside, and now he understood why Tryg had been having trouble with it.

It was fucking heavy.

"What do you have in there, your entire house?" he grumbled.

"Close to, yeah." Tryg ushered Isaac into the apartment and closed the door.

Thor dumped the luggage in the hallway and turned to face Isaac. They hadn't officially met yet, even though the three of them had skyped more than once. He was aware of Isaac's past, so he knew better than to try hugging him like he'd done with Tryg. He kept his distance and let Isaac come closer, shaking his hand when Isaac offered it.

"As you know, this is Isaac," Tryg said.

If Thor wasn't mistaken, Tryg's chest puffed up in pride, which was enough to make Thor smile again. "Pleasure to meet you, Isaac, and I have to say I admire you greatly. Choosing to spend the rest of your life with this asshole can't have been an easy decision to make."

Isaac chuckled, and the slight tension in the room relaxed.

"I don't see *you* having a gorgeous boyfriend," Tryg snarked.

"That's because not everyone is lucky enough to meet their soulmate."

Isaac's cheeks flushed, and he leaned against Tryg's side. Tryg automatically wrapped an arm around his shoulders and kissed his temple, and Thor's heart ached. He was happy for Tryg and Isaac, but he was also jealous. He had other things to focus on, thankfully.

"I'll show you the guest room," he said, a bit too roughly.

Tryg frowned, and Thor knew there would be a conversation in his near future. That was okay, even though it felt weird. He and Tryg talked on the phone, by texts, or they skyped. They rarely spent any length of time when they were actually together talking about feelings.

Thor showed them to the guest room, with Tryg rolling the luggage behind him, and left them there. He wasn't sure what to do or how to behave. He didn't have to cook, because they'd be getting takeout, and he'd already packed his bag for their flight to Brussels in the morning. The apartment was clean and neat, and he wasn't working right now. He'd even already booked the hotel and had bought an apartment in case they needed a safe place. He hoped the place was as pretty as it had looked in the pictures on the website.

Luckily for him, Isaac and Tryg emerged from the guest room after only a few minutes. Tryg flopped on the couch, pulling Isaac down with him and wrapping his arms around him again in what was clearly a protective gesture, even though he knew Thor was as safe a person as they came, at least for Isaac.

Isaac didn't seem to mind that Tryg always knew where he was and was always touching him. They were perfect for each other, as far as Thor could see—Tryg needed someone to protect, while Isaac needed to feel protected. It was a match made in heaven, even though it had started in hell for Isaac.

Tryg's need to protect people had pushed him into this job

in the first place, so Thor wasn't surprised that he was thinking about retiring, whatever Isaac thought about it. His need to protect was focused on Isaac now, on helping him find immortality and making sure he was okay, and that was exactly what Thor had wanted for him. He deserved to be able to relax and be happy.

"What about the mage you found?" Tryg asked.

Thor shook his head to get himself out of his mind. "I talked to him, actually. He started texting me and asking questions, then he called."

Tryg blinked. "He *called*?"

"Yep, but it was a blocked number, and I didn't locate him."

"Why not?"

"Because this isn't a job. We can't act like it is. Cecil is trusting us enough to agree to meet us. I didn't want to show him he *couldn't* trust us by trying to find out where he lives."

"What do you know about him, then?"

Thor had expected a small explosion, because Tryg was so obviously overprotective of Isaac, but maybe having Isaac in his life was helping him with more than just his need to protect.

Thor cleared his throat and tried not to smile. "Not much. I talked to him, and he seemed worried about why I was looking for someone who could make people immortal. I think he wanted to make sure I wasn't doing it for power or whatever."

"You told him about Isaac."

"Not in detail, but yes. I told him about you and how you met a human who didn't have the best start in life. Isaac will have to tell him more if he wants to, because it wasn't my story to tell, but I had to tell Cecil something and show him we're doing this for the right reasons. He sounds like a good guy, and the last thing I wanted was to send him running away by not answering his questions. Besides, you and I will be there with Isaac the entire time, and we'll meet Cecil in a public place the first time. It'll be okay. We'll make sure of it."

"Still. I'd feel better if you researched this guy a little."

"I thought about it. I even tried. But it's like he doesn't exist. I found mention of him in the gray web, and from what I read, he's damn good at what he does, but there is no personal information, nothing. The only thing that's talked about is his job, and it seems he's a good businessman who doesn't take a lot of jobs but who carries out all of those he does."

"I suppose we can't be any surer."

"I don't think so, no. But hey, I'll be there with the two of you, so no worries. You keep an eye on Isaac, and I'll keep an eye on Cecil. I'll make sure he doesn't even look bad at Isaac."

Isaac chuckled. "That might be exaggerated."

"But it's what I'll do if that's what you need." Isaac was family now, just like Tryg was, and Thor didn't have nearly enough family members to risk the safety of one of them.

CHAPTER THREE

Cecil took a deep breath that smelled of people and the city, of waffles and fries. He loved Brussels as much as he loved Paris, even with how different it was, or maybe because of it. Paris was tourists and art, and while Brussels was that, too, it had a more homely feeling, a feeling that he was where he belonged. That could be why he kept returning year after year, even though he didn't have an apartment there. He wanted to buy a place, maybe one of those Art Deco houses he'd seen in some neighborhoods, but he couldn't, not when his brother was still actively looking for him. He wouldn't be able to stand it if Fabrice shattered his dream of living here.

Which was one of the reasons he worried about their meeting. It had been easy to forget who he was until now, but he was about to meet Thorvald and his friends, and now that he was there, walking along the cobbled street that led to the Grand Place, doubts made his stomach churn.

What if this was an elaborate way for Fabrice to find him? Cecil had stayed out of his brother's way for hundreds of years, and his luck was bound to change eventually, especially since Fabrice was still actively trying to find him. Meeting in a public place was a way to try to make sure nothing would happen, but it wouldn't stop Fabrice. Nothing would.

Cecil needed work, though, both because of the money and because he was bored. This was the safest he could be, and he'd taken precautions, just in case Fabrice had something to do with this.

He finally stepped onto the Grand Place and looked

around. He was always in awe when he came here, and this time wasn't any different. The gray stone and the golden accents made him smile, and he chose a terrace that wasn't the usual coffee shop. He loved chai tea as much as anyone, but when he was in Brussels, he'd rather skip it. He wasn't about to order a beer, even though no one would have thought anything about it, so he got a coffee that was served with a small packet of speculoos, the spiced cookies he enjoyed so much.

Then he looked around again.

He didn't know who he was looking for. He knew Thorvald was tall and blond, and that he'd be with another tall and blond Viking, both of them probably wearing sunglasses. Isaac was an unknown, though. Cecil had no idea what he looked like, although he supposed it didn't matter. Two tall Vikings weren't going to be able to hide, even with the crowd of tourists walking through the square and stopping to take selfies and pictures.

Sure enough, he knew he'd found Thorvald when two tall blonds waded through the crowd to the center of the square. Cecil leaned back in his chair and observed them and Isaac, the smaller, darker man who was with them. He looked tiny next to the two giants, but Cecil doubted he was actually as small as he looked. He *was* thin, though, and he was clinging to his boyfriend's hand as if afraid the crowd would drag him away. His hair fell in front of his forehead, partially hiding one of his eyes, but when he leaned toward his boyfriend—Cecil couldn't remember the guy's name—his gaze shone with love, or at least, Cecil liked to think so. It had been so long since anyone had looked at him that way that he might have been wrong.

Thorvald and his friend looked around. Cecil had given Thorvald a vague description of himself, but with all the people walking around, he wasn't surprised that Thorvald hadn't noticed him yet. He grinned and picked up the single rose he'd bought on his way here, then held it up and waved with it until Thorvald's gaze stopped on him.

Cecil was relieved to see the smile playing on Thorvald's lips. Some people were too serious for their own good, especially when it came to immortality—which okay, it *was* serious, but if one was going to live forever, then they needed to relax, because it would be a hard forever if they didn't.

Cecil tried to relax, and when the trio was close enough, he handed off the rose to Thorvald with a flourish. "I thought this would make it easier for you to notice me," he said, forcing himself to smile in a way that hopefully looked natural.

Thorvald snatched the rose and smelled it. "It did, even though I wasn't expecting it." He held out his free hand. "Thor."

"Cecil, as you already know."

Thor nodded. "And these are Trygve, or Tryg, and Isaac. You can guess who is who?"

"It's easy enough. Why don't you sit down and order something to drink? I know you must be eager to talk about the reason you're here, but this is a beautiful day, and we're sitting in a beautiful place. We should enjoy it."

Cecil had made it his mission to enjoy life as much as he could, even though it was hard when he had to hide most of the time. He had no way to know when Fabrice would finally grab him, and he didn't want to have regrets.

Thor smiled, and God, he'd been gorgeous before, but now he looked angelic.

Well, if angels had piercings and short hair.

Thor wasn't quite what Cecil had imagined, even with the description he'd been given. The short hair suited him, as did the piercing in his lower lip, but the hoop of metal gave Thor an edge, made him look different from the good looks Tryg had, even though they could have been brothers.

He was sexy as hell, that was for sure, and Cecil didn't

know how to deal with it.

He swallowed and forced himself to focus on Isaac, since he was who they were here for. He leaned over the table and offered Isaac his hand, and Isaac took it. His hand was cold and dry, his fingers slightly loose as they shook. "Pleasure to meet you, Isaac."

"You're a mage?" Tryg asked.

Straight to the point. Cecil didn't mind.

Cecil slid his sunglasses down his nose so that the three could see his red eyes. "I am."

Isaac's breath hitched, but Thor leaned closer. "Cool color."

"They're the sign of magic."

"Well, I already knew you were a witch. You didn't have to flash us."

Cecil repressed the irritation at being called a witch. "I just didn't want it to be a surprise. People tend to not like it. I think they find it eerie and weird." Which it was. Not a lot of humans had red eyes, and most of them associated the color to demons and bad things. In some cases—like Fabrice—they were right, but Cecil liked to think he was a decent guy.

He turned his attention back to Isaac. "You want to be immortal."

Tryg cleared his throat. "Maybe we should avoid saying that kind of stuff in a public place."

Cecil nodded once to show he'd understood. "Okay. So, Isaac, you want to be *blond* like your man here."

Tryg glared while Thor guffawed. Even Isaac smiled, and Cecil felt himself relax.

He still didn't know if he could trust these people, but from his first impression, he liked them. Tryg was serious, although, given the way he seemed protective of Isaac, it made sense. Cecil wasn't sure about Isaac yet, but he liked Thor, and not just because he kind of looked like the Thor in the movie, except even sexier.

None of that would matter if they tried to hand him off to his brother, but he couldn't live his life afraid and waiting for something bad to happen. He needed this job to work, both for the money and because he wanted to help. Isaac seemed like a shy, nice man, and while Cecil would try to get to know him better before making his final decision, he was already leaning toward helping him.

Hopefully, Fabrice wouldn't find out about this, and if he did, it would take him long enough to get there that Cecil would be done before he arrived.

Thor wasn't sure what to think of Cecil. The rose had been fun, and it added to Cecil's cuteness and Thor's budding fascination with him. Thor hadn't expected it, and he enjoyed being surprised — as long as the surprise was a good one. He was looking forward to spending some time with Cecil and finding out just how making someone immortal worked.

Isaac was smiling when he answered Cecil's question about becoming *blond* like Tryg was. Thor had laughed out loud at that, and he liked the grin on Cecil's face as much as he liked how disgruntled Tryg suddenly was. He always took everything too seriously. He needed to smile more, to have more fun, and maybe now that Isaac was in his life, he'd finally manage that.

"You know what Tryg is," Isaac said. His voice was soft, like always, but Thor had already noticed his spine of steel. He hid it well, but it came out now that he wasn't afraid.

Cecil nodded. "I do. Thor told me. That's one of the reasons I agreed to this meeting, actually. I've never met a Norwegian, let alone two."

Thor laughed again. "Norwegians?" he asked.

"What? You might be, right? Do you know exactly where you were born? Although I guess things probably changed a lot since then."

"Can we please focus on this?" Tryg asked.

Thor would have teased Tryg about being too serious, but he understood why he was, and this wasn't the moment nor the occasion to push him.

"I was a sex slave," Isaac said, his voice soft—clearly he didn't want people around them to hear him. "I was homeless for a while, then a sex slave. I never had a home or a family. I never had anyone stand up for me or help me. *Until Tryg*. He came to kill the man who was keeping me chained to his bedroom wall, and even though he could have left me there, he took me with him. He freed me, and he protected me when that man's son tried to get to me. We fell in love. I don't want to lose the first thing, the first *person*, I love."

"You're young. You could be with Tryg for another fifty years, possibly more," Cecil said.

Thor wasn't sure why he was playing Devil's advocate, but he grabbed and squeezed Tryg's thigh when Tryg leaned forward, no doubt to interrupt the conversation. Isaac wanted this, and he needed to convince Cecil to help. He was the only one who could do that.

Tryg huffed and flopped back in his seat, but to Thor's surprise, he said nothing.

Isaac played with the edge of the empty cookie wrapper Tryg had gotten with his coffee. "Tryg is the first man I've ever loved, and the first man who's ever wanted me for more than my body, but he's also been lonely. No matter how long he's lived, it doesn't mean he was happy during those decades. I like to think I make him happy, and I want that to continue."

"Isaac," Tryg murmured. He reached out, and Isaac took the hand he was offering.

Yep, those two were made for each other.

"What if you two break up?" Cecil asked, apparently not

softened by the show of love.

"I won't stop loving him just because we're not together anymore," Isaac answered. "And the possibility of breaking up is always there in a couple, isn't it? Nothing can give anyone the certainty that they'll be together for years, let alone decades or hundreds of years. It doesn't mean people don't try and hope. And that's what I do. I hope, and I'll try for however long I have. Even if you tell me you can't do this, I'm not going anywhere. I just don't want to subject Tryg to the pain of losing me if there's even one chance for me to avoid it."

Thor held his breath and looked at Cecil, but instead of saying yes or no, Cecil asked, "I see. And you can pay?"

"I'll pay," Tryg said with a growl.

Cecil nodded. "What about him?" he asked, tilting his chin toward Thor.

Thor blinked. "What about me?"

"What do you have to do with this?"

"I already told you. Tryg is my best friend. He's my family, and now Isaac is, too. That makes it my responsibility to find you, especially since I'm the one with more experience researching." He leaned forward. "So? Are you going to do it?" That was the only thing that mattered.

Thor didn't care how cute Cecil was and how he was pretty sure he'd fall in love with him if he had the chance. He wasn't there to find himself a boyfriend, and Cecil was out of reach as far as he was concerned, at least until Isaac was immortal. But after that? Thor wasn't going to say no to getting to know Cecil and exploring the possibility of something happening between them.

Isaac came first, though, and so did Tryg.

Cecil didn't think Fabrice had sent Thor and his friends. He had no way to be sure—it wasn't like they'd tell him the truth if Fabrice was behind this, even if Cecil asked outright—but he wanted to believe it. He wanted to believe that the guy he found attractive and fun and caring really was all that. He wanted to believe the love he could see between Isaac and Tryg. He thought it was. It was too obvious to be fake.

But Fabrice had been sneaky before. He'd used some of Cecil's friends to get to him. Cecil couldn't put it past him. He'd learned never to underestimate his brother.

But regardless of whether Fabrice had or didn't have anything to do with this, Cecil wanted to take the job. He needed the money. He was bored. He felt like he was doing nothing with his life. And being immortal, that meant he'd wasted a lot of time. He didn't want that anymore, or at least, he didn't want that for a bit. He would have to go back into hiding soon enough. He could take a week, or a few days, to help Isaac. Isaac needed him, and while he could no doubt find another mage to grant him immortality, things were never this easy. Besides, Cecil was the best at his job.

There was a reason for that, of course, a reason he rarely explained. He believed he was going to have to explain this time. Thor and Tryg didn't strike him as the kind of men who would take his word without making sure that what he was saying was true and that they could trust him, as much as they could trust someone they'd just met.

They weren't the only ones who ought to be careful, anyway. No matter how much Cecil wanted to believe what he felt, he knew Thor, Tryg and Isaac about as well as they knew him. The last thing he wanted was to give in to his feelings and find himself in his brother's hands. His life depended on this.

He wrapped his hands around his mostly empty cup of coffee. "Do you have questions?"

Thor's eyebrows shut up. "Of course we have questions."

26

Cecil waved. "Go ahead and ask them, and I'll try to answer them as best as I can."

"How do you do it?"

This was a question Cecil was used to answering. Everyone asked it. Everyone wanted to know, but especially so when their lives were in the balance. He rarely told them the truth, but he suspected that Thor and Tryg wouldn't take a lie for an answer. They would no doubt check whatever answer Cecil told them, and if they discovered he'd lied, he would lose the job. He didn't want that to happen. He also didn't want to tell the truth, because people didn't usually like that answer. Maybe these two would be different, though. They weren't human. They were like him, probably more so than any other paranormal creature Cecil had come across.

Tryg leaned closer. "We're not doing anything with you until you answer that question. I won't even allow you to touch Isaac if you can't give me an answer I'll believe and that I can leave with."

Cecil raised his hands. "I will explain. But I need you to know that I'm not dangerous, or at least, I'm not dangerous for Isaac. This is a job, and I'll behave accordingly. I'm not about to do anything that could jeopardize the job or Isaac's life."

Tryg's eyes narrowed. "You don't know Isaac. Why would you care if his life was in danger?"

"I care because I won't be able to find another job if I mess this one up. You might have tried to research me, but I *definitely* researched you. I know how influential you two are in our world. You're great people. Others trust you, sometimes with their lives. It would only take one word from you, and all the good work I've done in the past decades would be lost. I need jobs. I need money. And I like to think I'm one of the good guys, too."

Thor cleared his throat. "Now that Tryg is done

threatening you, maybe you could explain exactly how this is going to work. I've done enough research to know that you did this in the past and that the people you gave immortality to are still alive and well, which is a huge plus in this case, but no one seemed to know *how* you did it."

This was it. The moment that would make or break this. It was the moment in which Cecil would find out if the three men in front of him we're as nice and genuine as he thought they were.

He interlocked his fingers over his knee and tried to avoid bouncing his leg. He didn't want Thor to realize how nervous he was. He didn't know why this was important to him, and he didn't want to analyze his feelings right now. It wasn't the right time or place. "It's tricky. It's not something everyone can do."

Thor snorted. "I know that. If becoming immortal was easy, everyone would do it, and I wouldn't have needed a week to find you. For some reason, you're special. You're one of the few who can do this. You're certainly the best. We wouldn't be here otherwise. I understand you probably rarely explain this in detail to your clients, but as you no doubt noticed, Tryg is very protective of Isaac. This isn't going to happen until he has the answers he needs and wants."

Cecil sighed. "I manipulate death."

The three men stared at him for what felt like an eternity but couldn't have been more than a few minutes. They were waiting for him to add details, but for some reason, the words were stuck in Cecil's throat.

Thor finally rolled his eyes. "You need to be more specific than that."

"I know. Just give me a few moments. I don't usually say these things out loud. It's . . . complicated."

"Manipulating death sure sounds complicated."

"That's because it is. It's a power that comes from my

mother. I've spent decades honing it and making sure I know exactly how it works, but explaining to someone isn't easy. I just don't have the words. What I can tell you is that my mother was a hag."

Thor's eyes widened. "A hag?"

At least he hadn't run halfway through the square yet. That was better than the last time Cecil had admitted this to someone. "Yes. You know what a mage is?"

"A witch."

Cecil wasn't going to slug Thor in the face, no matter how much he wanted to. Mages were commonly called witches by people who had no idea what they were talking about. Cecil was used to dealing with that, and he didn't go around punching people in the face. Or at least, he tried not to. That never ended well, considering he needed to keep a low profile so his brother wouldn't find him. "Mages aren't witches. We descend from paranormal creatures, usually through their union with humans. My father was a human, while my mother was a hag. She's who I get my powers from. She gave them to me when she died. *That's* what makes me a mage."

"So you're half human and half hag."

"Exactly. And hags have the reputation of riding people while they're asleep and creating nightmares, along with sleep paralysis. That's not all they do, though. In origin, people considered hags like benign nature spirits. They were spirits of healing and protection and controlled the waters of life and death. And what is death but a manipulation of life?"

Thor cocked his head. "It's a weird way to see things."

"It's not a way to see things. It's the way things are. The reason I can give Isaac immortality is that I can manipulate death, in this case, *his* death. I can't give any more details, because it's not something I can explain in words. I just know how it works. That's all you need, anyway."

Cecil had already given them more than enough, more so

than he'd ever given anyone else. He'd made himself vulnerable, and he hoped he'd been right in trusting Thor, Tryg, and Isaac.

Hags. Thor had expected a lot of things, but that wasn't one.

He'd stumbled upon a few hags over the years. Everyone in the paranormal world had. Hags were rare, probably just as much as draugr. That didn't mean they didn't exist, and Cecil was proof they did. Thor didn't have any kind of prejudice when it came to hags and their children. Draugr were often considered little more than zombies, and even when people realized they were human beings, they tended not to like them. Draugr didn't have good reputations, in part because of their powers. Thor could manipulate weather. He could walk in dreams. He could curse people and see their future. He could turn into smoke and shift into animals. He was immune to most weapons, and the only way to kill him was hard to find, close to impossible, actually.

Hags seemed to have the same reputation. Of course, the riding sleepers and bringing them nightmares bits didn't sound good, but Thor knew better than to believe everything he'd heard. Similar things were said about draugr, and few of them were true. He wasn't going to hold the fact that his mother was a hag against Cecil. It wasn't a choice on his part. Besides, Thor hadn't known Cecil's mother. As far as he knew, she'd been a delightful lady, nightmares notwithstanding.

"So, are all hags' children like you?" he asked, more curious than he probably should be.

"No. Hags' powers are left to their children. They have to decide who and when. My mother chose me when she was about to die."

Thor whistled. "I bet that it went well with your siblings."

Cecil chuckled. "About as well as you can imagine, which is one of the reasons I'm so hard to find. My half brother didn't take it kindly, and he's been trying to get to me ever since."

"It sounds like it's been a while."

"It has. But enough about me. Do you have other questions?"

Thor grinned. "So not all witches can do what you can do, right?" Thor had already realized that being called a witch annoyed Cecil. He should probably stop doing it, but he liked seeing the glint of anger in Cecil's eyes. It was as good a way as any other to have Cecil's attention on him. Thor should probably be ashamed of that, but he was seldom ashamed of anything. He, Tryg, and Isaac weren't there to flirt or to find him someone to warm his bed — but one thing didn't exclude the other.

Not that Thor was planning to get into Cecil's bed — not yet, anyway. Tryg would have his head if something went wrong because he'd seduced the mage who was supposed to make Isaac immortal.

"I am *not* a witch," Cecil snapped. "Witches don't have powers. They're usually humans trying to trick other people into believing whatever bullshit they're selling. I might use gemstones and candles and whatever else some witches use, but my powers and what I do have nothing to do with what they try to convince the world is real."

Yep, he was definitely annoyed. Thor felt slightly guilty at needling him, but it wasn't his fault Cecil was adorable when he was flustered. His eyes shone with passion, probably not too different from the way they looked in bed.

And Thor needed to stop thinking about Cecil in bed. That way lay madness, and it wasn't something Thor could face now.

"How long do you need to be ready to do this?" Tryg

asked. He glared at Thor, clearly wanting him to stop dicking around.

Thor winked at him. He could restrain himself for a bit. *Probably. Hopefully.*

Cecil relaxed and turned his attention to Tryg. "A few days at least. I know what I'm doing, and I've done it several times, but I need to put together the ingredients I use to stay focused and to give my power the boost I need to do this."

"You made it sound easy earlier when you were talking about this."

"It's not easy. Like Thor said, if it was, everyone would do it. It's easier for me because I've done it many times, and I could do it right now with none of the ingredients I usually use. I would spend the next few days in bed, though, and not in a fun way. The ingredients I use make my job easier, and thanks to them, I need less time to recuperate when I'm done. Of course, this doesn't concern you. You don't have to worry about me."

Tryg looked guilty. Thor knew he was pushing so hard only because he cared so much about Isaac. Most people would find him ruthless, though, because they couldn't know about the depth of his feelings. "I don't want to make your life harder. I just want Isaac to be in good hands, whatever that entails. Like you said earlier, he's young. He can wait a few weeks or even a few years."

Cecil chuckled. "He won't have to wait that long. I only need a few days. But this is where it gets complicated."

Thor didn't like the sound of that, and from his expression, neither did Tryg. "Complicated?" he asked.

"In a way. I need my ingredients, but they're not the only things I need. I'll have to be sure that the place where we're going to do this is safe. I need people to guard over me while I'm doing it because I'll be dead to the world during that time. I can't afford to be distracted while I'm manipulating death, and as I mentioned before, some people would think nothing of using this moment in which I'm most vulnerable to get their hands on me. We can't afford for that to happen. *Isaac* can't afford for that to happen."

Thor wasn't surprised. He might have been making light of the situation, but he realized how hard this would be on Cecil. It surprised him that Cecil didn't have his own way to be sure nothing happened to him while he was manipulating death. "We'll do it."

Cecil blinked. "What?"

"Tryg and I will watch over you and Isaac when you're doing this. I'll even take care of the aftercare, if you need it."

Cecil's cheeks flushed. "I tend to be weak once I'm done. Sometimes I'm confused and unsure of where I am or who is with me. That's why I need protection, and that's why I probably shouldn't have told you about this."

"You can trust us."

"How am I supposed to know that? We just met. You're as wary of me as I am of you. But it's kind of too late for me to be careful. I guess I'll have to deal with whatever happens when it happens. I hope the consequences won't be too great for me to deal with."

Thor didn't like that Cecil didn't trust him, but he understood why. Cecil was right. They didn't know each other from Adam. As far as he knew, Tryg and Thor might be planning to hit him upside the head while he was doing his manipulation thing and then sell him out to the best offer. No amount of promises would change that. Only time would—time, and seeing that Thor and Tryg—and Isaac—hadn't lied.

"We'll pay you right away," Tryg suddenly said.

"You don't have to. I usually take payments after I'm done. I realize it's probably not the best idea, but I wouldn't feel right if something happened and I wasn't able to give my clients what they want from me," Cecil said.

This man needed someone in his life, someone who would

make sure nothing happened to him. He was too nice for his own good, and eventually, someone would take advantage of that. Thor was stunned that no one had already.

And he would do what he could to make sure that never happened.

CHAPTER FOUR

Cecil was way too excited for this. It was true he didn't manipulate death often, so that probably accounted for part of the way was feeling. He enjoyed using the powers his mother had left him. It made him feel closer to her, even though she wasn't alive anymore. She'd chosen him to leave them to instead of his half brother, and that thought always make Cecil feel special, not only because he could now use her powers but also because she'd thought so well of him to leave them to him. She could have chosen his brother since Fabrice was older and they'd been closer than she'd been to Cecil, but she'd selected him.

He also didn't get to manipulate death often because he was picky about who he did it for. Some mages weren't, and it usually brought trouble. Cecil didn't want trouble. He already had enough of that as it was.

So the day had felt like a treat in more ways than one. The fact that Thor would be there only added to the feeling.

After their meeting, Cecil had used the new information he'd gathered to do more research about the trio. There weren't as many bad things in their past as he would have thought, considering how long they'd lived. They'd sometimes chosen the wrong people to take out. Sometimes, they'd had to deal with families and business associates. But all in all, they were good men, just like Cecil had thought. He'd be safe with them. He was sure of that.

And he was sure of the fact that he already had a crush on Thor.

It was ridiculous. He'd talked with the man for all of half an hour. Even with the research he'd done, he couldn't say he knew Thor, not personally. He didn't know how Thor was first thing in the morning. He didn't know if Thor was a considerate person or lover. He didn't know what Thor liked or disliked, or if they were in any way compatible. No, the only thing he knew right now was that Thor was sexy, which he supposed was better than nothing. Still, it wasn't exactly the best basis for starting a relationship. Not that he and Thor would be in a relationship anytime soon.

Cecil needed to see where this day went to before he allowed his brains and his heart—and his dick—to run away with this crush. He might never see Thor again after today was over.

A knock on the door made Cecil jump. He'd been expecting it, but that didn't mean he wasn't nervous. There were several ways in which the manipulation could go wrong. Hopefully, nothing would happen to Isaac, but the thought was enough to make Cecil wonder if this was a good idea.

He shook his head. It was a good idea. He had experience in this. He could do it. He had before, and he would in the future. He was a good mage, and he'd show that to Thor and his friends.

He was wearing loose and comfortable clothes that wouldn't hinder his ability. He couldn't help but notice how Thor's gaze slid over his entire body when he opened the door. He knew the clothes were more revealing than what he'd worn three days ago when they'd met, but it wasn't on purpose. He needed to feel comfortable for everything to go well, and that was what they all wanted—even if it made him uncomfortable right now. He wouldn't care once he was working, anyway.

Cecil stepped aside. "Welcome. Please come in."

Thor, Tryg, and Isaac obeyed. The three of them looked

around, no doubt curious. Cecil had told them he needed a safe place to do this, and while he could have chosen a place that would have been new to both him and them, he preferred using the apartment he rented in Brussels. He knew he would be safe there, and it had been quicker than looking for another safe apartment that his brother wouldn't find.

"Is this where you live?" Thor asked.

"For now. It's temporary."

Thor's expression was thoughtful. "I get the impression that a lot of things in your life are temporary."

That was too close to the truth for Cecil to be comfortable discussing it. "Isn't everything temporary?"

Thor arched a brow. "You're the guy who deals with immortality. You tell me."

Cecil gestured toward the hallway. "Why don't we head to the guest room, where I'll be doing this?"

"You don't want to talk about this."

"I don't have the time to talk about this, not if you want Isaac to be immortal by the end of today."

Cecil led the way to the guest room. In the middle of the small table in the center of the room, he'd already gotten everything he'd need ready. He'd lit the candle he would use to focus. He'd scattered gemstones around it, and he'd started burning herbs. The room felt very much like a witch's shop would, but what Cecil was going to do was nothing like what would happen in such a place.

He sat on one side of the table and crossed his legs. He gestured at Isaac to mirror his position on the other side of the table. The candle was in the middle, separating them, but Cecil placed his hands onto the table, palms up in a clear invitation.

"What's the candle for?" Thor asked.

Cecil huffed. "You and Tryg can sit against the wall."

They obeyed, with Tryg sitting on Isaac's side, slightly

behind him. He was close enough to grab Isaac if something happened, which was no doubt the reason he'd picked that spot. Thor, on the other hand, had sat close to Cecil. Cecil had no idea why, but he hoped it wouldn't make the manipulation difficult. Cecil needed to focus, and that wouldn't be easy with Thor so close to him that Cecil could smell his lemony aftershave.

"You didn't answer my question," Thor pointed out.

"You don't need to know how it works."

"Maybe not, but what if I want to?"

Cecil would have to answer that, wouldn't he? "The main reason to have a candle there is that I need to focus on something, and it's easy to focus on the flame."

"What about the stones?"

Cecil sighed. Of course Thor had more questions. "They help with focus, too. I usually hold at least one of them in my hand and stroke it."

"How is that supposed to help you focus?"

"How am I supposed to focus with you asking a hundred questions?"

Instead of being cowed by Cecil's words, Thor looked amused. "You can't blame me for being curious."

"Not for being curious, no. But I can blame you for asking so many questions."

Isaac chuckled. "If I didn't know better, I'd think you two had a history."

Cecil supposed he and Thor were acting as if they did. Maybe there was more to this attraction than he'd thought. He hadn't spent too much time wondering if Thor felt the same way he did. It had felt like a moot point. But maybe it would be worth exploring once this was over.

Cecil cleared his throat. "Ready to begin, Isaac?"

"So we're going to ignore this," Thor murmured.

Cecil was tempted to confirm that they were, but that

would be against the point he was trying to make. Instead, he smiled at Isaac and pointedly looked at his offered hands. Isaac's cheeks flushed, and he reached for Cecil. "Do I have to take both of them?"

Cecil shook his head. "One is enough."

Isaac slid his fingers against Cecil's left palm. Cecil nodded, and without looking at the table, reached for the gemstones. He closed his eyes and felt his way around them until he found the one that felt right in his hand. He rubbed his fingertips over it and slowed down his breathing. Thor's scent wrapped around him, but instead of breaking his focus, it helped him get into the zone. He had no idea why, and he wouldn't investigate now. Now, he had a job to do, and he was going to do it.

Thor didn't understand what was going on. He had no idea how this worked, and he didn't need to know. That didn't mean he wasn't curious as hell.

As far as he could see, the only thing Cecil was doing was holding Isaac's hand and stroking one of the gemstones. Cecil had closed his eyes, and so had Isaac, even though Cecil hadn't told him to. There was a tension in the room, something that felt electrical on Thor's skin. It tingled, but it wasn't unpleasant. Thor couldn't help but wonder if it was a sign of Cecil's power. Was he supposed to feel it even though he wasn't part of this manipulation thing?

Thor and Tryg exchanged a glance. Thor was surprised Tryg hadn't yet tried to intervene. As overprotective as he was of Isaac, it was hard to believe he didn't want to pull Isaac away from Cecil. Although maybe it was believable. He knew this was Isaac's only chance at immortality. They both did, and neither of them would do anything to ruin that chance. Besides, Isaac or Cecil might get hurt if Thor or Tryg tried to come between them. They had no clue how the manipulation worked exactly, no matter how Cecil had tried to explain. They couldn't afford for either Cecil or Isaac to get hurt just a because they didn't know what was going on.

He was stunned when light started shining from Isaac and Cecil's linked hands. "Is that normal?" Tryg asked.

Thor didn't know how to answer that. "Probably."

"Probably? Are you sure you're trying to reassure me?"

Cecil opened an eye and glared at Thor as if he'd been the only one talking. "I need to focus," he said through gritted teeth.

Thor gave him what he hoped was the winning smile and raise his hands. "Sorry," he mouthed.

Cecil closed his eye again, and the light coming from his hand flared.

And that was the only thing that changed for the next hour.

Thor ended up leaning against the wall. It was more comfortable than being there in the middle of the room staring at Cecil and wondering what was happening. Thor wasn't sure what he'd expected to see, but it wasn't this, especially because *nothing* was happening. There was light, sure, but that was it. No mumbling, no gestures, nothing.

Then it was over.

Or at least, Thor thought it was over. Cecil let go of Isaac's hand and leaned back, almost falling to the floor. Thor hadn't been expecting that, but he caught Cecil before he hit the floor. He cradled Cecil against his chest and slipped behind him so that Cecil could lean against him better. "Everything okay?" he asked.

Cecil groaned but nodded. "I'll be fine."

"You're sure? Because you don't look so hot."

"I feel like I should be offended."

"Oh, trust me. I wasn't commenting on your appearance. You're still sexy as hell. You just look like you could use a nap."

Cecil chuckled. "I do feel like I should probably sleep for a bit."

Tryg cleared his throat from the other side of the table. "Is it done?"

"You couldn't wait five more minutes to ask?" Thor asked with a growl. He loved Tryg, he did, and he understood why Tryg was so anxious about this, but couldn't he let Cecil rest for a bit before bothering him?

"It's okay," Cecil said. He leaned forward, and Thor wrapped his arm around his waist to make sure he didn't fall face-first on the table. "It's done."

That was it. That was all the explanation Cecil gave Tryg before flopping back against Thor's chest. Tryg blinked at him and opened his mouth, no doubt to ask more questions, but Thor glared at him. Tryg snapped his mouth shut and dragged Isaac into his arms. Thor nodded in satisfaction and turned his attention back to Cecil. "Is there anything you need?"

"Rest, mostly, although I wouldn't say no to a snack."

"I can do that." Even though he would have to let go of Cecil to manage it. Although, since Cecil seemed to need rest, maybe Thor could help him lie down somewhere and take care of the food while he was sleeping it off.

"I'm immortal now?" Isaac asked.

The only reason Thor didn't growl at him, too, was that no one could growl at Isaac and not feel like an asshole afterward. Isaac probably felt different than he had only a few hours ago, and the slight trembling of his voice betrayed how nervous and probably frightened he was. He needed reassurance, and this time, it wasn't something Tryg could do. No matter how hard Tryg might try, Isaac needed to know what was happening from Cecil, since Cecil was the one who had done this.

Cecil blinked as if he'd already been half asleep. Maybe he had. It certainly felt like he was falling asleep as he pressed his back against Thor's chest. "You're immortal," he confirmed.

That was when all hell broke loose.

The room's window was covered by a curtain, and while Thor had noticed it, he hadn't thought about it twice. He'd known Cecil thought he was in danger, but he hadn't thought the danger would find them there. He wasn't sure why since this was his job, but he didn't have time to berate himself for not being more ready to face this.

The window broke, and glass was flying everywhere as someone burst through it. Thor had time to push Cecil to the floor and roll them so that Cecil was under him before the shooting started—fucking *fireballs*—but it left him without a way to see what was happening. There was nowhere he could stash Cecil to make sure he wouldn't get hurt while he took care of the threat. There wasn't a closet in the room or any other piece of furniture that would be big enough for that.

So even though Thor's instinct was to stand and face the fireball shooter, he ignored it, kept his hands on Cecil, and turned both of them to smoke.

He noticed Tryg doing the same thing with Isaac, and he relaxed, knowing the four of them were safe. It was easy to decide what to do then, and Thor headed back to the window. Broken glass dangled from the frame, but it was easy to float out of it while the shooter looked for them in the room, especially with the curtains and pillow burning. It was hard to resist the urge to look back and see who the shooter was, and since the shooter had no idea what was happening, Thor felt it was safe enough to do so.

He faced the window and peered inside. The shooter was dressed entirely in black, like in one of those bad military movies. Even his face was covered by a black hood, although that probably hadn't been a bad idea, considering the pieces of glass that glinted on it. The shooter had avoided getting hurt by the glass by covering his face. The problem for Thor was that he had no way to identify the guy. He couldn't ask Cecil if he knew who it was, because he couldn't speak in this form. He could have reached out to Cecil's mind, but he could feel how confused Cecil was, so he probably wouldn't be able to give Thor an answer.

Their best option was to leave. Thor could let go of Cecil as soon as they were far enough for him to be safe, but he already knew he wouldn't do that. He couldn't. He'd promised Cecil that he would take care of him and make sure he was okay while Cecil did his job and made Isaac immortal, and he'd do that. It had nothing to do with the fact that he liked Cecil or that he thought Cecil was gorgeous—or at least, that was what he tried to convince himself of as he floated away from the window.

Cecil wasn't sure he'd ever felt this lost. He didn't know what was happening—or why he didn't seem to currently have a body.

He searched his memory even as he looked at the man standing in what had been his guest room. He was renting the apartment, goddammit. The landlord was going to be pissed when he saw the busted window.

Cecil couldn't help but wonder what it meant about him and his state of mind that the first thing he was thinking of was the broken window rather than his well-being. He was okay, though. He thought he was, anyway. He couldn't tell if anything hurt, because he wasn't a physical being right now, but he'd be able to as soon as this stopped.

If only he knew what *this* was.

It was weird. He'd never thought about not being

corporeal. It wasn't something he could do, not even with the magic he'd inherited from his mother. He'd heard about the power draugr had of turning into smoke, though. He hadn't thought he'd ever be caught up in that, but it looked like he'd been wrong. That would only happen once he faced the truth of what was going on.

His brother had found him.

Dammit. Cecil had thought he'd be safe in Brussels. He'd only been there a week, not even that. How had Fabrice found him? Cecil had been careful, as careful as he always was. He'd been so sure he hadn't left clues behind. His brother shouldn't have known he was in Paris, either. Cecil didn't think Fabrice had followed him from one city to the other, but that still didn't tell him how his brother had found the apartment he was renting.

Are you okay?

Cecil startled at the voice in his head. He supposed he shouldn't have, considering the fact that he often talked to him himself. Still, the voice in his head was usually himself. He wasn't used to having someone else there, even though he recognized the voice. *Thor?*

Cecil had no idea if he was doing this the right way, and he held his breath as he waited for Thor to answer.

Who else could it be? Do you often have people talking to you in your head?

Cecil rolled his eyes, or he tried to anyway. He didn't have eyes at the moment, and he wasn't sure how this worked. *You're not as funny as you seem to think you are.*

I'm hilarious, thank you very much. Are you okay, Cecil?

Cecil took the time to assess himself. Nothing hurt, although that probably was because of his lack of body right now. He was surprised to realize he felt tired, because how could he be tired if he didn't have a body? The manipulation on Isaac had taken its toll on him, though, and he realized how lucky he'd been that Thor had been there to save him from Fabrice. Cecil would be in his brother's hands right now if he'd been alone. He didn't want to think about what Fabrice would have done to him. He already knew, and in detail—too much detail He'd seen enough of Fabrice's victims to know he didn't want to be one of them.

I'll be okay. He can't see me, right?

No. The only thing he'll see if he looks this way is a bit of smoke.

That was reassuring. Cecil didn't know how this worked, but Thor did, and Cecil trusted him. He wasn't sure why or when it had happened, but he did. *Good.*

Hold on. I need to talk to Tryg.

Cecil looked around. He suspected Tryg and Isaac had become smoke like he and Thor had, but no matter how much he tried to see them, he couldn't. He didn't know where they were, but Thor seemed to. He floated to the left, then stopped. Cecil didn't see or hear anything, and he startled when Thor's voice talked in his mind again.

You're coming with us.

Cecil wasn't offended by how sure of himself Thor sounded. He didn't want to stay there. He didn't want to face his brother. That never ended well, and Cecil was already tired enough from the manipulation on Isaac. Fabrice would clean the floor with him if he tried to face him. *Where are we going?*

Instead of answering, Thor asked, *do you know who that is?*

My brother.

Are you sure? You can't see his face.

Cecil wished he wasn't sure. *I am. Fabrice is the only one who would do this.*

You're going to have to tell us what happened with your brother. We need to know what we're up against.

Cecil was shocked at the way Thor assumed he would stick with them. He wished he could, but he didn't want to put them in danger, especially Isaac. Isaac might be immortal now, but that wouldn't help him if someone shot or stabbed him. He deserved the chance and time to enjoy the immortality Cecil had worked so hard to give him. That wouldn't happen if Fabrice found them. He'd hurt Isaac, Thor, and Tryg to get at Cecil. Cecil would never forgive himself if something happened to the three men. They'd trusted him to make Isaac immortal, and he had. He wasn't going to be the reason Isaac lost it. *I can take care of Fabrice on my own.*

He could almost hear the snort in his mind.

Sure you can.

I can. I might be weak right now, but this isn't the first time Fabrice found me.

Maybe not, but from what you are, saying, it does seem to be the first time you won't be facing him alone.

Cecil's chest felt tight. No one had ever tried to save him from Fabrice. Everyone had always been too afraid of him to try. Cecil didn't blame them. Hell, *he* was afraid of Fabrice on the best of days. He knew exactly what Fabrice could do, and he knew he was too weak to face his brother and win. *We can't face him. He's too strong.*

Tryg and I are stronger than you seem to think.

I never said you weren't. But I know Fabrice. I know what he can do, how he can hurt you.

But you don't know what Tryg and I can do. Okay, we're leaving. This isn't the right moment anyway. But we're not done talking about this.

Cecil sucked in a breath, or at least he felt like he did. *You can leave me halfway to your place. That way Fabrice won't be able to follow you there. You should leave town as soon as you can. Fabrice is bound to find out who you are and where you're staying eventually.*

I'm not leaving you anywhere. You're coming with us.

You have to realize it would be safer if I didn't.

And you have to realize that's not going to happen.

Cecil wasn't sure how to feel about that. He didn't want to be left alone in a city where he didn't have other allies. He didn't want to have to run on his own again. But he also didn't want Tryg, Thor, and Isaac, to be hurt, not on his behalf. *He's going to find us.*

And we'll face that possibility once it presents itself. You can stop arguing with me, Cecil. You can't become physical again if I won't allow you to, and I won't, not as long as we're not safe. You're coming with me, whether you like it or not.

This man was infuriating. *I don't want him to hurt you or Isaac.*

He won't.

You can't know that. You don't know him.

He could be Lucifer himself, and I wouldn't change my mind. No matter who your brother is or what he can do, we're not leaving you to face him alone. You're going to have to start getting used to that.

Why are you doing this? You don't know me. We're not friends. I'm just a guy who helped you get what you needed, and you don't owe me anything.

Tryg and Isaac disagree, and I agree with them. You researched Tryg and me. You know what we do for a living. You also know that we try to go after the monsters, the men and women who don't deserve to live.

You don't get to decide who deserves to live.

If you think that, we're going to have a problem, but now isn't the right moment to talk about this. What I was trying to say is that your brother has been hunting you for what sounds like a while. I don't know why, but I doubt it's because you're a bad man. Chances are, he *is, and that makes him my business.*

CHAPTER FIVE

Thor was angry. He still didn't know why he cared so much for Cecil, but it didn't matter. Cecil was in danger, and Thor's job was to help people in danger. That meant he was going to help Cecil, whether or not Cecil wanted it.

And he didn't seem to want it.

Thor wasn't that surprised. From the little he knew about Cecil, the man didn't want other people to get hurt because of him. That was probably one of the reasons he'd wanted to meet in Brussels. It was obviously not the city he lived in regularly, although Thor doubted that he lived anywhere on a regular basis, not with his brother hunting him. Cecil had to be used to bouncing from city to city in the attempt to lose his brother and stay safe. It wasn't a way to live, but especially not for a man as nice and sweet as Cecil.

Thor turned in the direction of the hotel where he, Tryg, and Isaac had been staying. He and Tryg had talked about it, and Isaac had agreed. They wouldn't abandon Cecil to himself. They wouldn't have even if they didn't like Cecil as much as they did, because that wasn't who they were. They were protectors, as Isaac's rescue had shown. That wasn't going to change right now, especially not with the crush Thor had on Cecil. His crush didn't matter, though. Cecil was the one who had given Isaac and Tryg what they most wanted, and that meant he'd earned Thor's eternal gratitude.

Not the hotel.

Thor frowned at the sound of Tryg's voice in his mind. *Why not?*

We have no way to know how Cecil's brother found him. He might have followed us, as far as we know.

Thor hadn't even thought about that. It was obvious he hadn't worked in the field for too long. *How could he have known about this?*

I don't know. He probably doesn't, but I'm not willing to risk it. I don't think you are, either. We need to keep both Isaac and Cecil safe, and that means leaving everything behind.

That wasn't going to be a problem. Neither Tryg nor Thor ever traveled with important things, with things they couldn't replace. They'd also made sure they had their cell phones and tablets on them in case they needed them. There would be nothing in the rooms at the hotel that could lead to them.

My place? Thor asked. He was glad they'd decided to go to a hotel when they got in town. He would have been disappointed if he'd had to give up his new apartment. He might have just bought it, but he liked what he'd seen of the city so far, and he was looking forward to exploring it — once Fabrice had been dealt with.

Cecil's place was further away than Thor was used to floating to. He really had to get off his ass and start working out again, and it looked like that was what he would have to do.

He was tired by the time he slid under one of the windows of his new apartment. Tryg and Isaac were right behind them, and they shifted back to their human forms almost at the same time. Cecil has been quiet during the time they'd traveled, and Thor realized why when the man almost fell on his face as soon as he was human again. Thor managed to grab him before he hurt himself, and he held him up. "Are you okay?"

Cecil chuckled. "I've been better."

"You'll be safe here."

"Will *you* be?"

Thor had no answer to that. He understood where Cecil was coming from, but that wasn't going to make him change his mind. The three of them — he, Tryg, and Isaac — knew what was happening. They knew what they were facing. They'd all agreed that they wanted to do this, to help Cecil, and hopefully, to get him his life back. "We will be," he answered. Cecil was waiting for him to say something, so he had to. "I just bought this place. No one knows about it except for the three of us. Even if your brother somehow finds out where we are staying, he won't find us, because it wasn't here."

Cecil blinked. "You bought an apartment?"

"I did."

"Why?"

Thor shrugged. "Why not? I have the money, and I like what I've seen of the city in the past few days. I wanted to come back . . . to have a place to stay when I did. There's no way your brother found out my name, not unless you wrote it down somewhere. Do you use a computer?"

"Of course I do. But I always make sure not to write down my clients' names. I know Fabrice would be able to track me through that, and I'm not about to risk it. He won't find anything, not even if he somehow unlocks my computer to get in my files." He sighed. "Although I do wish I could go back to get my computer. It was new, dammit."

"We're leaving for the night," Tryg said.

Thor turned to look at him and Isaac. "Let me know when you get where you're going."

"Wait. What?" Cecil asked.

"Tryg and Isaac are going to go out in the city to ask questions, see if they can find out where your brother is," Thor explained. "Tryg won't tell either of us where he and Isaac will spend the night, just in case. We'll stay in contact, and we'll meet again tomorrow, but for today, it's safer for everyone to separate."

Cecil's eyes were huge. "I'm so sorry. I never meant for this to happen."

Thor patted his arm. "You have nothing to blame yourself

for. We decided we wanted to get involved, and we already knew we'd have to separate. Don't worry. All four of us will be okay." He turned to face Tryg again and nodded at him. "The only thing I'm sorry about is that we didn't get to spend near enough time together."

Tryg smiled. "Let's solve this problem, and we'll take a vacation together when it's done. Maybe the four of us?"

Thor glared at his best friend, but Tryg was already shifting him and Isaac to smoke. They slid out from under the same window through which they'd come in, and Thor turned his attention back to Cecil. He was still holding him up, but now he took his first good look at him since they'd been shot at.

Cecil was still wearing the loose, light clothing he'd been wearing for the manipulation, but it wasn't as white as it had been. Even though they'd escaped the apartment almost as soon as the shooter had entered, they'd rolled around on the floor for a bit, and there had been glass everywhere. Cecil's clothes were now streaked with dirt and blood. "Are you okay?" Thor asked.

"I'm fine."

"You don't look fine."

"It's nothing too bad. A few cuts here and there."

Thor swore. "Come on. I'm pretty sure I have stuff to clean you up in the bathroom."

"I thought you just bought the apartment?"

"I did, but I also paid someone to buy the bare necessities. There should be clothes in the bedrooms and food in the kitchen. So we won't starve, and we won't have to leave the house for a few days. We can hide and wait for your brother to leave."

Thor gently guided Cecil toward the guest bedroom. He was relieved to see towels hanging and soap and shampoo on the sink. There was even a tub, and Thor suspected Cecil wouldn't say no to a bath. First, though, Thor had to clean his wounds.

He got Cecil to sit on the toilet seat, then looked around for the first aid kit. Cecil had several cuts on the bottom of his feet, but luckily, they shouldn't be so bad he couldn't walk. Thor turned on the water in the tub while he worked on cleaning the blood off Cecil's skin. He didn't cover the cuts, since Cecil was going to take a bath, but he made sure they weren't bad enough that they might need stitches.

"All done," he said once the last cut was clean. He patted Cecil's knee and rose from his crouch. "I'm going to leave you alone so you can bathe."

"I can shower."

"You could, or you could take advantage of the fact that there's a tub right there and that I've already started filling it. Take a bath, Cecil. Try to relax. There's no way for us to know when we'll be able to do that again, so you should do it while you can. I'll be in the kitchen. I'm going to put a snack together for you." He should probably offer to help Cecil get into the bath, but he wasn't sure he'd survive seeing Cecil naked right now. They both needed some time to cool down and relax, and Cecil wasn't going to be able to do that with Thor drooling all over him.

Cecil was going to fall asleep. The bath wasn't the best place for that to happen, though. The last thing he needed was to drown in the sweet-smelling water. It wouldn't be a horrible death, especially next to what Fabrice would do to him if he ever managed to catch him. That didn't mean Cecil was looking forward to it.

But he was confused.

He didn't understand why he was there. He was grateful to Thor for saving him from Fabrice, of course, but anyone else would have dumped his ass on the closest corner and run out of there. Cecil wasn't proud to admit that he probably would've done that if he'd been in Thor's shoes.

But he wasn't in Thor's shoes, and he was grateful for that. He'd be halfway dead by now if he'd been.

That didn't help him understand what to do now. He didn't want to put Thor in danger, and that was what his presence was doing. The best thing for him to do would be to leave, but he doubted Thor would allow it. The man had a protective streak a mile wide, and it was coming out to play now that he knew Cecil was in danger.

Cecil hauled himself out of the bath. He dripped water all over the floor, and he had to catch himself on the edge of the tub so he wouldn't break his head open on the floor. He was too tired to do this. He should have stuck with the shower, but the bath had sounded so good. He'd wanted a bit of time to relax and wash the grime and blood off his skin. Now he had, and he was a little more ready to face Thor.

Cecil left the bathroom wrapped into a soft towel. He didn't want to put on those dirty clothes again, but he wasn't sure he'd have an alternative. It wasn't like he could go home to the apartment he rented and get a bag. Even though he doubted Fabrice was still there, he knew Fabrice would monitor the place until he was sure Cecil wouldn't come back. It would be stupid to go, no matter how much Cecil wanted his things back.

So towel it was, or at least, Cecil thought so until he got to the bedroom. He hadn't expected the small pile of clothes waiting for him on the bed. He vaguely remembered Thor telling him about the clothes in the bedrooms and the food in the kitchen, but he hadn't thought about that until now. It was hard to believe that Thor was this prepared to face an assassination attempt. Of course, he couldn't be sure Fabrice wouldn't have killed Cecil. He needed him, and what he needed him for wouldn't work if Cecil was dead.

That was why Cecil was a bit confused about Fabrice shooting fireballs. If he'd manage to hit Cecil, to kill him, he would have lost what he'd been trying to gain over the past decades. Maybe he'd just been trying to scare Cecil. Cecil wouldn't put it past him. Fabrice was an asshole, always had been. And it would never change.

Cecil dropped a towel on the floor and reached for the clothes. They were simple — a pair of sweats and a black t-shirt, but it helped to put them on. They made Cecil feel less vulnerable, which was exactly what he needed right now. He didn't know what was going to happen tomorrow, how he was going to escape from Fabrice's claws again, but that wasn't something he had to think about now. He *couldn't* think about it now, not if he wanted to be able to get through the rest of the day and the evening without breaking down. He didn't want that to happen in front of Thor.

He knew he wasn't like Thor, or Tryg for that matter. He had no idea how to do this. The only way he knew how to fight Fabrice was running, which was what he'd been doing for the past few decades. He was sick of it, but the way he felt about it wasn't going to change anything. He couldn't allow Fabrice to get to him, not if he wanted to stay alive. Fabrice wouldn't kill him right away, because he needed him, but eventually, that was exactly what would happen.

Instead of leaving the bedroom and trying to find Thor, Cecil stepped outside on the balcony. The night was already falling, and it made him wonder how long he and Thor had been smoke. He also had no idea how long he'd been in the bath. The fact that he hadn't fallen asleep in the warm water was a small miracle. It would have been ironic if Thor had saved him from his brother only to let him drown in the bath.

The air was cool, and Cecil took a deep breath. It helped him feel better as much as the bath had. He was starting to realize he was safe, and his body was relaxing on its own. He looked out at the sky, smiling at the sight that greeted him. He loved the *Atomium*, even though it was nothing more than huge silver balls linked together. He liked the lights on it, the way they moved and changed as the night grew darker. They made him feel at home even though he wasn't.

"I thought you'd come downstairs."

Thor's voice behind him startled Cecil. He jumped a little, and Thor reached for him as if trying to reassure him. Cecil would have let him, but instead of touching him, Thor took a step back.

"Sorry about that. I didn't mean to scare you."

Cecil shook his head. "I'm fine. Or at least, I'm realizing that I'm fine."

"The bath helped?"

"More than I thought it would. Thank you."

Thor rubbed the back of his head. "I didn't do anything." He cleared his throat. "I found some food in the kitchen, or we can get takeout."

Cecil frowned. "Wouldn't that go against the whole hiding thing?"

"I doubt your brother followed us. Even if he tried, we were much faster as smoke than he could have been even in a car or on a bike. He hasn't found us. I'm sure of that." He grinned. "So? Pizza?"

Cecil couldn't help but smile back. "Pizza here? I mean, I'm sure you can find a good one, but I'm not in the mood for waiting. Unless you know a place?"

"I don't. It's my first time here."

"Then whatever you have will be enough. I'm not picky." Cecil couldn't be, not when being on the run could mean some days, you didn't eat at all.

Thor nodded. "Pasta it is, then. Maybe you can tell me about your brother while we're eating."

Cecil didn't want to talk about Fabrice. He didn't even

want to think about him, but he owed Thor at least this. "Wouldn't want to put you off your food."

Thor snorted. "Trust me. It's going to take a lot more than this to put me off my food."

Cecil knew he was probably right. The main reason he didn't want to talk about him was that he hated even thinking about it, and most days, he tried not to. But again, he owed it to Thor. Thor needed to know what he was going against if he wasn't going to change his mind about protecting Cecil. Cecil was afraid that Thor would decide he'd be better off out there, but it was a risk he needed to take. For the first time in a long time, someone was trying to help him, and he wouldn't hold it against Thor if he changed his mind. He'd already given Cecil more than most people had.

Thor waited until they were both sitting at the small table by the kitchen with steaming plates of pasta in front of them to ask, "Why is your brother so bent on killing you?"

Cecil sighed. "How do you know he wants to kill me?"

Thor arched a brow. "He came in shooting fireballs. That tells me he doesn't want to talk."

"You're right. He doesn't. He also doesn't want to kill me, though."

"Could have fooled me."

"He needs me alive."

"Why?"

That was the question Cecil didn't want to answer. "I told you about my mother."

"That she was a hag."

"Yes, and that she died. When she died, she had to choose whether to take her powers with her or leave it to one off-spring. She left it to me." And that had been the start of Cecil's problems.

Thor wasn't sure what the problem was, so he stayed quiet and waited for Cecil to explain.

Cecil sighed and poked at his pasta with his fork. "Some paranormal creatures can choose whether to die with their powers or pass them on."

Thor had known that. Draugr weren't part of that group of creatures, but he'd been alive long enough to know about it, even if Cecil hadn't already told him when they'd first met.

"So my mother passed them onto me. I'm still not sure why she chose me instead of any of my siblings, but the *why* doesn't matter. It's not like she can explain herself. What *does* matter is that Fabrice wasn't happy about it."

Thor pointed his fork at Cecil. "He wants your power."

Cecil gave a tight nod. "He does. He's been after me ever since our mother died. He's the oldest, and he feels the power should have gone to him. I can't say he's wrong, not entirely. I never wanted this power."

"What power are we talking about here? Is it the one of manipulating death?"

"It's one of them, yes. The power of manipulating death comes along with other things. I told you that hags in origin were nature spirits that were thought to protect and guide, and in some cases, heal."

"Does that mean you have a healing power?" Because Thor could understand why Fabrice wanted the power, if that was the case. It would come in handy. Hell, it would come in handy even for Thor. Thor didn't work in the field, but that didn't mean people didn't try to kill him every so often. Having someone who could heal him with him would be a good thing, especially if combined with what Cecil was saying about the power of protection.

"It's a small one. It's not strong or anything. And the protection I was talking about is more protecting small villages and whatnot from other paranormal creatures. I can also control nature, like make trees move, things like that. I don't think the reason Fabrice is still hunting me for the powers is because he needs them, though, not anymore."

"Why, then?"

"He hates me."

When Cecil didn't continue, Thor put his hand out and reached for Cecil's hand, giving it a quick squeeze before taking his back. He didn't want to make Cecil uncomfortable, just to let him know he wasn't alone. "Why do you think he hates you?"

"I don't think he does. I *know* he does. I told you, he thought he should have been the one to get our mother's powers. He never forgave her for giving them to me, and he never forgave me for accepting them."

"Could you have said no?"

"No, but Fabrice has never been objective when it comes to this. He saw it as a personal offense, and he's been trying to get me to transfer our mother's powers ever since, mostly the one about manipulating death."

"And you never have."

"I never will. The thought of what he could do if he could do that is terrifying. I'm not saying I'm perfect, but I never use the power to hurt anyone."

"Your brother would?" Thor didn't need Cecil to confirm that to know it. Just the fact that Fabrice had barged in shooting fucking fireballs was proof of that. He hadn't cared who would get hurt. He'd only cared about hurting Cecil, and that told Thor everything he needed to know about the man.

"He would. After I wouldn't give him the power, he started hunting me and other people. When he captures them, he torments them until they give him whatever power he's after. Then he kills them. He's been accumulating powers ever since our mother died. I don't know what kind of powers he has now, but I'm pretty sure manipulating death isn't one of them. I would have heard about it."

"He could get it from someone else, though? Right?"

"He could. It's not a common power, but others have it."

"But he's obsessed with you."

"Yes. Like I said. He's never forgiven my mother or me for what happened, and I don't think he'll be happy until he can take the power away from me."

"Even if it means torturing you?" Again, Thor already knew the answer to that. Cecil's brother was obsessed with him and with hurting him as much as he thought he'd been hurt. The fact that he was planning to kill Cecil in what was obviously an overreaction, especially with how long it had been, told Thor what he needed to know. Fabrice was a dangerous man, a dangerous *creature* who didn't pause for anything to get what he wanted. From what Cecil was saying, Fabrice had been torturing and killing people for decades. Nothing would stop him from getting to Cecil.

Thor was relieved that he and Cecil had met. He could too easily imagine Cecil facing his brother alone, and that terrified him. He'd be afraid for anyone, but after what Cecil had done for Isaac and Tryg, it was especially scary. Cecil was a good man with a power a lot of people would abuse. The fact that he hadn't was a small miracle in itself, and the fact that he was doing all he could to keep it away from his brother was another.

Most people probably would have given in a few weeks or months after Fabrice has started hunting them. Thor suspected that the reason Fabrice wanted Cecil's power, in particular, was that it would thrill him to take it away from his brother. He wanted to get back at their mother and Cecil, even after all those years. That showed just how determined he was, and he wouldn't stop until he had what he wanted — Cecil's death and his powers.

"He won't stop for anything or anyone," Cecil confirmed.

He had eaten nothing from his plate, and Thor gently pushed it toward him. "You need to eat."

"I am. I'm not very hungry."

Thor doubted anyone would have been hungry after the brother had tried to shoot them down, but that didn't change the fact that Cecil needed all his strength to continue escaping from Fabrice. "I understand, please try. We don't have a way to know if or when Fabrice will find us, but I want both of us to be well rested and well fed when or if it happens."

"He'll find us." There was hopelessness in Cecil's voice, and Thor didn't like it. He wanted to do something, anything to help Cecil, but right now, he didn't know where to start.

He needed to check in with Tryg to make sure he and Isaac were okay. Once that was done, he could focus on researching Fabrice and trying to guess what his next step would be. Thor didn't think Fabrice would quit, and that meant that he had to be ready for when Fabrice finally found them. That would be near impossible since he didn't know what kind of powers Fabrice had, though. "Is there any way to find out what your brother can do?"

"I've been trying. I want to be prepared when he finds me, but no one is talking. They're afraid of him, and with good reason. I probably wouldn't have talked, either, if our roles were reversed."

Probably not, but Thor would have to find a way around that. He wasn't going to allow Cecil to be hurt, and right now, their best option was to stay hidden. "Can I ask you why you let things get this far?"

Cecil's eyes narrowed. "Are you asking me why I didn't kill him when I had the chance?"

"It's what I would have done."

"But I'm not like you. I'm not a professional killer. I'm not a *killer* . . . period. I couldn't have done it, not even with all the powers in the world. I just want him to leave me alone and to be able to live my life in peace."

Thor had seen enough of Fabrice to know that wasn't going to happen. It would be his life or Cecil's, and he knew what he wanted to happen.

"Besides," Cecil continued. "Our mother's powers don't work on him, not the way they work with everyone else."

"So you've tried?"

"I tried talking to him and in his dreams in the beginning. I can dream-walk to him, but I can't influence what he's dreaming about. He always knows I'm there, too. I haven't tried manipulating his death, but I doubt the result would be different."

"What are you going to do, then?" Because as much as Thor could try to help Cecil, that would only work if Cecil agreed to it.

Cecil linked his fingers together on top of the table. "I'm going to stop running."

Thor blinked. "What does that even mean? He's going to kill you if he manages to catch up to you."

"I know. I haven't thought about it in detail yet, but I'll find a way. I don't want to die, and I don't want to kill Fabrice, but I'm not an idiot. I know something has to give, and we can't live this way forever."

Thor knew Cecil didn't want to hurt his brother, but if things came to that, Thor wouldn't back down from doing it himself — however Cecil reacted to it. He didn't care if Cecil resented him after it, as long as Cecil was alive to hate him.

CHAPTER SIX

It took Cecil a moment to realize where he was when he woke up the next morning. The conversation with Thor last night hadn't lasted long after Cecil had declared that he was done running. He knew Thor was alarmed by that fact, but it wasn't going to change his mind. He didn't know what would happen, or how he'd manage to convince his brother to stop hunting him, but he'd find a way. He had to. Seeing Thor with Tryg and Isaac had made Cecil realize how alone he was. Even with his few friends checking in on him regularly, Cecil was lonely.

He couldn't see them. He put their lives in danger, and he wasn't going to allow that to happen. He knew that Fabrice would pounce on the opportunity of hurting him if he could. That was why Cecil hadn't met with any of his friends in at least five years. He talked to people, but it was only people he didn't know, people Fabrice couldn't use to get to Cecil.

He wanted more. He *needed* more. He was living his life — if he could even call it a life. Spending time alone wasn't that much of a burden, but that was only because he liked it. Sometimes, though, he wanted a friendly face, a nice chat, maybe even a hug. God, he couldn't remember the last time someone had hugged him. He needed human contact, no matter how hard he'd been trying to ignore that lately.

But how could he seek that out when he knew he'd be putting those people in danger? Even Thor had already realized Fabrice wouldn't stop for anything, and he'd barely seen him five minutes if even that. What did Cecil think he could do?

He hauled himself out of bed with a sigh. He wished he could stay in it all day. It was comfortable, and he didn't have to confront the world from there. He could pretend everything was okay, and maybe that he and Thor were an item. It was a pointless dream, but it was just a dream, and Cecil didn't feel the need to stop thinking about it. He doubted Thor saw him as anything but a man to protect. He was Thor's next project, and that was okay. Cecil was terrified, and he could too easily imagine how worse he'd feel if he were alone to face this.

But he wasn't alone. That meant something to him, and he didn't know how he'd ever be able to thank Thor.

Maybe he could get breakfast ready. From what he'd seen last night, Thor could *eat*. He'd cleaned off his plate and Cecil's, and Cecil suspected he'd still been hungry after that. He probably wouldn't say no to a nice breakfast. It was the least Cecil could do. He didn't know what would happen today, but from the little he knew about Thor, he was pretty sure Thor wasn't going to let him out of his sight.

But when Cecil got downstairs after washing up and putting on the clothes he'd worn yesterday after his bath, he found the small kitchen table already crowded, both with food and people.

Isaac looked up as he entered. He smiled, and Cecil smiled back automatically. Then his eyes widened as he took in the amount of food on the table.

He hadn't expected Tryg and Isaac to be there this morning. He knew Thor had called them last night to make sure they were okay, but he hadn't said anything about them coming back so soon. It looked like they'd visited a supermarket and a baker before arriving. The table was crowded with everything, from *pains au chocolat* to croissants, from thick slices of bread and butter to *hagelslag*, from waffles to *speculoos* cookies. Thor was the one responsible for the waffles. He was in the kitchen, his back to Cecil, delicious-smelling steam rising from the waffle maker.

Cecil cleared his throat. "Good morning."

Isaac's smile widened. "Good morning. Come sit with me. I'm going to need help to finish all of this."

"I doubt we'll be able to do that, even in two, or in four."

Isaac's cheeks flushed. "Tryg decided to spoil me. We were talking about typical foods from around here, and he realized I hadn't had any of them."

"And he decided to buy all of them at the same time?" It was impractical, but Cecil couldn't deny it was also adorable. Tryg was taking care of Isaac, making sure he was comfortable and happy, and that was what Cecil wanted in life. He didn't have anyone who took care of him like this. He wasn't sure he deserved it, but if he didn't, then he wanted to be the one who took care of someone this way.

"We're not going to stay here long enough for him to try them one at a time," Tryg pointed out.

Cecil's gaze moved to Thor. Thor was coming closer, carrying a plate full of waffles. He smiled at Cecil, and Cecil looked down at the empty plate in front of him. He didn't know how to behave or what to think about the way Thor was looking at him. He was probably only thinking that he wished he'd never met Cecil, or at least, that Cecil's life wasn't a mess he'd been drawn into. He was too good of a man to abandon Cecil to his destiny and Fabrice, and he wouldn't say anything about it, but Cecil couldn't believe Thor was eager to get involved in this.

Cecil licked his lips. "Where will you go?"

"We're going to stick together," Thor said. "Or at least for a while. We can travel to the safe house we decided was the best place for us to be right now and stay there for a while at least."

"Or we could separate, like we decided last night," Tryg

said. He probably didn't want Isaac to be in danger, and Cecil understood that. He didn't want Isaac to be in danger, either.

"Even if we do separate, we should meet at the house. We're going to have to come up with a plan to get Fabrice to stop hunting Cecil, and it'll be easier to do that if we're together. Besides, I'm pretty sure Isaac is about ready to strangle you. He's been spending too much time with you, and *only* with you. I get that you two are in love and happy and whatnot, but he needs friends, and I'm not talking about your dick."

Isaac's cheeks became even redder. "I don't mind being with him."

Thor snorted. "I sure hope you don't, because you're never going to get rid of him. But that wasn't what I was saying. It's great that you and Tryg found each other, but you need friends, friends who aren't Tryg. You *deserve* friends after everything you've been through."

Perhaps now wasn't the right moment for Isaac to make friends. Cecil couldn't help but think that, even though he didn't say it out loud. Instead, he grabbed a waffle from the plate and dropped it on his, then proceeded to drown it in syrup. "None of you have to come with me."

"We don't have to, but that doesn't mean we won't," Thor said.

Cecil and Thor hadn't talked about it much, but Cecil was convinced more than ever that he couldn't put those three men's lives in danger. That was exactly what was going to happen if they came with him, though. "He won't stop because I'm not alone," he pointed out.

"I don't expect him to. He's been after you for decades. I don't think anything short of death will stop him by now."

And since Cecil didn't even want to consider killing his brother, Thor was going to do it for him. Thor didn't have to say it for everyone at the table to know it.

Tryg cleared his throat. "I think we should go to my cavern in Italy."

Thor shook his head. "Nope. I was thinking north. I have an apartment in Scotland."

Tryg wrinkled his nose. "An apartment? In the city?"

"I know how much you like dark caves, but not all of us do, and I want Cecil and Isaac to be comfortable. Trust me, you'll like it. We'll be able to keep an eye on the paranormal community there and make sure Fabrice doesn't find us."

Cecil didn't know why the three of them were including him in this. Thor had told him he wasn't going to leave him alone, but Cecil didn't understand why. They didn't know each other. He might have given Isaac immortality, but that had been business. This wasn't, not anymore. "Why?" he croaked.

Thor blinked. "What do you mean?"

"Why are you helping me? Why are you doing this? Why are you putting your life, and Isaac's and Tryg's, in danger for someone you don't know?"

Thor wasn't sure how to answer that. He wasn't sure why he was doing it, except that he didn't want Cecil to get hurt. *Why* was anyone's guess, but Thor wasn't looking forward to explaining to Cecil that he had a crush on him, especially not with Tryg present. He'd never hear the end of it, and he wasn't sure he was ready to deal with it right now. They had better things to focus on, like planning a way to get Fabrice to back off from his brother.

"We are protectors," Tryg answered before Thor could think about a better way to put things.

"You're professional killers." Cecil looked as confused as he had before.

Tryg's answer hadn't convinced him, and to be honest, that

was because it *wasn't* convincing.

"That doesn't mean we can't protect people." Tryg sounded offended.

Thor understood why. The fact that they were professional killers was true, but even though they killed people for a living, they always made sure the people they took care of were on the wrong side of the law — on the wrong side of humanity. Thor hadn't accepted a job in decades, and everyone Tryg had killed recently had deserved it a hundred times over, like the man who had kept Isaac prisoner. Isaac would still be in that man's hands if Tryg hadn't accepted the job of killing him. It wasn't a loss for anyone. If anything, the world was a better place without that man in it.

"They *are* protectors," Isaac intervened. "Tryg saved me. He protected me."

Cecil sighed. "I understand that, but I'm not sure it applies to me. I'm no one's prisoner. I might be in danger, but it's nothing new, nothing I can't face myself, and most of all, you don't owe me anything."

"I owe you my future," Isaac pointed out.

"You paid me for it, and handsomely. That means you don't owe me anything, not anymore."

"Why don't you want us to help you?"

That was exactly what Thor was wondering. He doubted Cecil would answer the question if he'd been the one to ask it. Maybe with Isaac asking it, he would.

Cecil played with this fork. He didn't look at Isaac as he answered, "It's not that I don't want help. I do. I'm not a fool, and I realize that if I ever tried to take my brother on alone, it won't end well for me. I'm not suicidal. I'm not looking forward to the confrontation. But that's exactly why I think I should do this alone. I know my brother, and I know how powerful he is, even though I haven't faced him in a while. I don't want anyone to get hurt, least of all you. You just became immortal. Your life before was horrible, and you deserve to be happy. You deserve to take advantage of the immortality I gave you, and that won't happen if you get hurt, or worse, because I was too selfish to say no."

No matter how little Thor liked Cecil's answer, it made sense. Cecil might spend most of his time on his own, but even though they hadn't had the occasion to talk much, Thor had been able to see just how caring the man was. He cared about Isaac, even though he didn't know him. He wanted Isaac to have a good life, and he was afraid of Isaac getting hurt because of him.

Thor's crush kind of made sense now.

It made sense and reinforced Thor's decision to make this work somehow. He wanted to get Cecil out of trouble, then to date him. He hoped Cecil would say yes because he wanted to rather than because he needed to. That was why Thor wanted to wait, but he wouldn't have a chance to date Cecil if Cecil's brother killed him.

"Isaac isn't going anywhere near your brother," Tryg said with a growl. "Thor and I will take care of Fabrice, not Isaac."

"But he's right here with us," Cecil pointed out.

Thor couldn't help but fear Cecil really was suicidal. Why was he trying so hard to change their mind?

"And he's here to stay. I'm not about to let him out of my sight, not when I just found him. But he's not going to go anywhere near your brother, because I'll make sure he doesn't. Thor and I, on the other hand, are professionals, like you said before. We could create a paranormal bodyguard's business and have no problem finding clients."

Thor blinked. That didn't sound like a bad idea. He and Tryg had been thinking about retiring, mostly because Tryg's job was too dangerous and Thor wanted to spend more time with his best friend, but they were both aware that they'd get bored within a week. This paranormal bodyguard thing sounded like a good way to keep busy, make money, and stay out of trouble — mostly.

"You can be our first client," Thor said. Cecil couldn't say no to that, right?

Cecil frowned. "What are you talking about?"

Thor grinned. "The paranormal bodyguard business. It's a good idea, and you can be our first client. You can even pay us, if it makes you feel better, but I'm not going to get offended if you don't. It won't change how hard I'm going to work to keep you safe." He wasn't doing it for the money.

He didn't have to say that for Tryg to know it. He didn't miss the way Tryg looked at him, but thankfully, Tryg didn't ask awkward questions. Thor knew the questions would come eventually, but as long as it happened later, he was fine with it.

"Now isn't the moment to talk about this." Tryg raked a hand through his long hair. "We need to start planning. Cecil, you should get used to the idea that we're not going anywhere, especially Thor. We'll stick by your side until we know you're safe, so the sooner that happens, the sooner you can get rid of us."

Cecil opened his mouth, but Tryg cut him off. "Now that it's decided, what's the next step?"

Thor liked where things were going. Since Cecil protested every time that he and Tryg suggested they wanted to protect him, they could ignore his protests and do what needed to be done. He smiled at Tryg. "We shouldn't wait until Fabrice comes to us. That would give us the worst hand."

"We could use Cecil as bait."

There wasn't a good reason for Thor to feel like he'd just eaten lead rather than waffles. "No."

Cecil opened his mouth again, but both Thor and Tryg ignored him. Tryg wrinkled his nose. "Why not? It would be the easiest way to get Fabrice to us. If we plan it, we will be in control of the encounter."

"But Cecil could be hurt, so that's a *no*."

"But—"

"Let's stop talking about it. That plan is out of the question."

"We must make a choice, Thor. Don't let your little head do the thinking for you. We can't afford it in this case."

Thor wanted to strangle Tryg, but he managed to keep his hands where they were. "Fine. We'll consider it if we have to, but not one second sooner. And stop talking about my little head."

"What are the two you doing?" Cecil asked. He didn't sound angry, but rather confused.

"Trying to decide what our next step is," Thor answered, then turned to Tryg again. "You're right that we should draw Fabrice to us, but I don't like pulling Cecil into it. I also don't like the fact that we know next to nothing about Fabrice. We need more information before we decide anything."

"He's going to suspect Cecil isn't alone anymore."

"He probably already knows that. That's okay, though. He's going to think Cecil is with me, but he has no idea the two of you exist," Thor said, pointing at Tryg and Isaac. "That means I can focus on protecting Cecil and making sure nothing happens to him while you two do some research. You don't have to hide out with us, even though it wouldn't be a bad idea. You can go around and ask questions, get us the answers we need before we make any kind of decision about what's going to happen."

Thor didn't like the fact that they wouldn't be together, but he and Tryg had both known this was going to happen, even though they'd tried to ignore it. Even if they did end up reuniting at Thor's apartment in Scotland, it wasn't going to be right away, but at least they'd have answers. They needed a plan, and for that, they had to know exactly what they were facing.

They were separating.

Cecil had known it would happen. Thor and Tryg had talked about it at breakfast in front of him and Isaac, and while Cecil had wondered if they were really going to do it, he was glad he'd had the warning. He didn't like knowing he and Thor would be alone, because it would be effortless for Fabrice to hurt them if they were, but on the other hand, he was happy that Isaac wouldn't go anywhere near Fabrice. He hadn't been lying when he told Isaac he wanted him to be happy. Isaac deserved it, probably more than anyone else Cecil had ever known.

Cecil didn't like the fact that Tryg and Isaac were going to poke around in Fabrice's life and history, but nothing he'd said had changed their minds. The three of them — Thor, Tryg, Isaac — were focused on liberating Cecil from Fabrice. Cecil had no idea how they were going to manage that, considering he hadn't in all the decades since his mother had died, but he'd given up trying to convince them to leave. They weren't going anywhere. That much was obvious.

Tryg and Isaac were supposed to join Thor and Cecil in Scotland once they were sure Fabrice didn't know where Cecil was, and once they had something to share about Fabrice's past and present. Cecil already knew he would have to face at least one interrogation from Thor, but that was okay. Thor already knew everything there was to know about Cecil and Fabrice and the past they shared. The only things Cecil could add were details, things he couldn't remember right now.

At least he and Thor would be out of danger. If they managed to get to Thor's apartment without Fabrice realizing what was happening, Cecil didn't think Fabrice would be able to find them. Fabrice didn't know he was with Thor. Cecil and Thor hadn't known each other until a few days ago. Even if Fabrice got his hands on Cecil's records or found out in any other way that someone that hired Cecil for a death manipulation, the person who had actually hired Cecil was Tryg. Thor wasn't mentioned anywhere. He wasn't the one who had paid Cecil, and Cecil knew the email account from which Cecil had received that first email was a temporary one. It was true that Cecil and Thor texted and called each other, but Thor had reassured him that no one would be able to get into his phone records. If they did, they wouldn't be able to trace it to him or to link him to the apartment.

Cecil hoped Thor was right.

"Everything will be okay," Isaac said.

Cecil blinked at him. He wasn't sure why Isaac felt the need to reassure him. Maybe he looked like he needed it. He certainly felt like he did, but he always tried not to let it show how he felt in his expression. He was failing today. "I know."

Isaac cocked his head. "Do you?"

"Of course I do. Tryg and Thor have everything under control, don't they?"

"They do. He likes you, you know?"

Cecil didn't have to ask what Isaac was talking about, but he did anyway. "Thor?"

Isaac nodded. "Yes. I don't know him very well, but Tryg wouldn't be friends with him if he wasn't a good man. Besides, he helped Tryg and me when we needed it."

"I never thought either of them where bad men."

"But you didn't want us to help you."

"Only because I don't want you to get hurt. My brother will stop at nothing to get to me. Or anyone."

"We're all aware of that. We still want to help."

Cecil had enough of this argument. Nothing he could say would change those three men's minds. He didn't want to change their minds, anyway. He needed help, and he knew it. He just hoped no one was going to get hurt on his behalf.

Isaac patted Cecil's arm. "Thor will keep you safe. You should look at this like a vacation of sorts. When was the last time you had enough time to relax? When you had nothing to do?"

Cecil snorted. "Vacations are supposed to be relaxing. How am I supposed to do that when I know my brother wants to kill me?"

Isaac grimaced. "I realize it's a bit more complicated than I was trying to show. It's probably going to be next to impossible for you to forget that Fabrice is looking for you. Obsessing over Fabrice isn't going to help you, though. You need to be at your best when Tryg and Thor decide it's time to face him. That's not going to happen if you can't sleep because you're thinking about all the ways he's going to torture you."

Cecil barked out a laugh. He liked that Isaac wasn't mincing his words. "I'd like to see you try to forget that your brother wants to torture you."

"I had to go through something similar."

Cecil's stomach dropped. He didn't know the details of Isaac's past, but he knew enough to have a good idea what had happened to him, or at least, to imagine it. "I'm sorry."

Isaac shrugged. "You have nothing to be sorry for. I don't expect you or anyone else to walk on eggshells around me. My past is what it is, and I'm learning to deal with it. It's not easy, but I want a normal life, or at least, as normal a life as I can have. You shouldn't have to be too careful about what you're saying around me. What I'm trying to say is that I know how it feels when you know someone wants to hurt you. I know how it feels always to be afraid that the moment has come. To expect it. To count the seconds until it comes. It's not the same situation, but fear is fear. The fact I had it worse than you doesn't mean you have it easy."

Cecil was in awe of Isaac. He was sure that in Isaac's place, he'd be curled up in a corner. But instead, Isaac was facing life as it came—he was doing what he could to help Cecil. He was strong, stronger than anyone Cecil had ever met. "Thank you."

Isaac's cheeks flushed. "I was just trying to say that no matter how hard it is, you need to focus on the good things. Stop thinking about your brother and what's going to happen. Obsessing over it isn't going to help anyone but him."

He was right. Of course he was. Thinking about Fabrice never helped Cecil. Cecil had always had to think about him because he'd been alone. He'd never been able to let his guard down.

But now he was. He wasn't alone anymore. Thor was there, and he would protect him. Cecil was sure of that.

He was looking forward to it. He didn't know how a relaxing vacation worked. He'd never had one. He wasn't sure how relaxing this was going to be, but he'd be with Thor, and they'd be alone. They'd have to stick together in the apartment, and that meant they'd spend a lot of time together, talking and getting to know each other. As far as Cecil was concerned, that would be the highlight of this situation.

Maybe he really could make it. Maybe he had a future after Fabrice. He'd never let himself think about it because he hadn't thought it possible. But maybe he could make the best out of this thing. Maybe he could make friends and even get a boyfriend.

He wasn't blind. He'd noticed how Thor looked at him. He didn't know if exploring that was the best idea, but he'd had enough of living in fear. Fabrice had controlled Cecil's life until now, and Cecil had let him. He'd been a loner because he was afraid Fabrice would hurt anyone he cared for. He was still afraid of that, but he knew Thor could defend himself.

He wanted to give himself a chance at having a normal life,

exactly like Isaac was doing. He wanted to come out of this alive, well, and not alone.

It looked like this was his chance to have that.

CHAPTER SEVEN

Thor had no idea what time it was when he and Cecil got to his apartment in Dundee in Eastern Scotland. They'd flown to London, and he'd been tempted to stay there. He had an apartment in the city, and he loved spending time there. He knew it would be too easy for Fabrice to find them there, though. London was a big city, and that wasn't always a good thing. The big city meant a lot of eyes and paranormal creatures who might see them and report to Fabrice. Not that Thor's apartment in Scotland was in the middle of nowhere, because he liked spending time in cities more than he did in the country, but it would be easier for him and Cecil to hide. The paranormal community where they were headed was much smaller than the one in London, and that lowered the chance of being noticed.

Thor turned him and Cecil back into their human form as soon as they were through the window. Thor seldom used the door when he was there, or when he was in any of his apartments. Being able to become smoke had its advantages.

"Stay here," he told Cecil.

Cecil looked at him with wide eyes. "Is something wrong?"

"Not that I know of, but I'm going to make sure."

"Thor," Cecil started. Thor shook his head and disappeared into the dark living room.

He needed to make sure they were alone. The apartment's alarm was still on, and it hadn't been tripped, but Thor had no idea what Fabrice could do. From the sound of it, he was a formidable magic wielder, so he might be able to sneak into the apartment without the alarm or Thor noticing. Thor wasn't going to put Cecil's life in danger just because he was overconfident.

The place was empty, though. It smelled of dust and emptiness, and it was dark, but it wasn't anything Thor hadn't expected. He returned to the living room, pleased to see that Cecil was still by the window that led to the balcony. He looked wary, but he relaxed when he saw Thor coming toward him. "It's safe?"

Thor nodded. "As safe as any place can be, considering."

"I suppose I needed to make my peace with that."

Thor abhorred the fact that Cecil was used to being in danger. He was used to spending time alone and hiding. While Thor's life, especially in the past few decades, had included a lot of hiding, he'd chosen it. He'd been the one who'd decided he wanted to spend so much time alone in his apartment. Cecil had had no such choice, and Thor wanted to change that. No one deserved to spend their life hiding, especially when they hadn't done anything wrong. And Cecil hadn't. He was a good man—a man Thor was grateful he'd stumbled upon. He couldn't wait to see where things between them would go—if they went anywhere in the first place. Thor had no idea what Cecil thought of him or what he wanted beyond being safe, but maybe spending time with him while protecting him would help him get the hint. He didn't like not knowing, but in this case, pushing would make things worse and harder on everyone.

Thor shook his head to clear his thoughts. "Come on. I'll show you to the guest room." And he'd make sure to show him where the master bedroom was, just in case. Cecil needed to know that if anything happened while they were in the apartment, but the fact that he might use the knowledge for something that had nothing to do with danger was thrilling.

Thor took his thrills where he could these days.

Thor walked down the hallway and opened the guest room door. "The room has its own bathroom, so you don't have to worry about sharing with me." Which was a pity, because Thor wouldn't have said no to Cecil stumbling upon him while he was in the shower. "You'll find towels and spare clothes in the drawers, but let me know if you need anything else. I'm going to have to go out grocery shopping. If I remember right, I didn't leave a lot of food the last time I came here."

"You spend a lot of time here?"

"Not recently." Which meant going grocery shopping was probably a good idea. Even if Thor *had* left something to eat in the apartment, he doubted it would still be edible by now.

Cecil flopped to the edge of the mattress. "I'm fine with anything. Just buy what you need or what you want, and I'll eat it."

He looked like he could use a nap. "Why don't you shower and rest while I'm out? Or you can explore the apartment. That's fine, too."

Cecil gave a tired smile. "You don't seem to care about the fact that I could snoop around."

"There's not much of my stuff here, so I doubt you'd find anything even if you did snoop around. You're welcome to it, though. I have nothing to hide."

Cecil blinked. "Sometimes, I can't help but wonder if you're real."

Thor decided to take a risk and reached for Cecil. He skimmed his fingers along Cecil's cheekbone and gently cupped his cheek, rubbing his thumb on the soft skin. "I'm very real, Cecil."

Thor dropped his hand before things could get awkward and turned around. He cleared his throat has he headed for the door. "Like I said, you have free run of the place. Stick your nose wherever you want. I'll be back as soon as I can."

Thor was grateful for the cool air when he stepped onto the

balcony. He should probably have used the elevator, but this was easier, and he wouldn't have to unlock the door and disarm the alarm. Cecil would be safe, but that didn't mean Thor could allow himself to waste time.

He poofed into smoke and moved over the railing and down the apartment building. He'd bought the top floor because he hadn't wanted to be boxed in by the neighbors. It had cost him a little more, but it was worth it, and he loved the apartment as much as he loved the others that he owned scattered all over the world.

He'd chosen this building because it was in the center of the city. Everything was close by, so it only took him five minutes of floating around to get to the parking lot. He lowered himself at the back of the lot, made sure no one would notice him, and turned back to his human form. He stretched a bit, not used to spending as much time in his smoke form as he'd been lately, and headed toward the store.

He bought too much stuff, especially because he and Cecil might not stay for long. He wanted to spoil Cecil a bit, though, and okay, maybe to show off — as much as one could show off when grocery shopping. Fabrice might find them tomorrow, and they'd have to run, but in the meantime, Thor wanted Cecil's life to be as normal as possible. He wasn't sure normal was something he could offer, but he was going to try.

He went back to the apartment and snuck in through the balcony before turning back to his human form and dumping the grocery bags onto the counter in the kitchen. The apartment was dark, something he hadn't expected. Maybe Cecil felt too intimidated to make himself at home. It wasn't a thought Thor enjoyed.

He put everything that belonged in the fridge inside — after dumping the wrinkly lemons and the open jar of mayo he found there — before going to find Cecil. He didn't have to look far. Cecil was in the living room, asleep on the couch. He was clutching the remote control of the TV, but he hadn't turned it on. He'd curled himself into a tight ball, his free hand resting next to his cheek on the pillow. He looked like he might be cold, so Thor grabbed the blanket he'd left on the back of the couch and draped it over Cecil's body.

He was right. Cecil needed the rest, and Thor wasn't about to wake him up. He had no reason to.

He went back to the kitchen to unload the grocery bags. It was late afternoon, and Cecil would probably be hungry once he woke up. Thor might as well make himself useful and get dinner ready. There was nothing else he could do for Cecil right now, anyway.

Cecil woke up to the smell of something cooking. It didn't happen often. He'd always lived on his own, and he wasn't a good cook. He didn't want to risk poisoning himself when he couldn't get to a healer because whoever he found might sell him out to Fabrice. He survived on takeout and ready meals, but this didn't smell like one of those. No, it smelled like home cooking, and Cecil's stomach rumbled.

He looked around, trying to understand how long he'd been asleep. It had been long enough that Thor had come back with the groceries and had started cooking. It was dark outside the window and in the living room, but that didn't help Cecil understand how late it was.

He knew draugr preferred the dark. They could go out during the day and even in the sun, but their skin burned easily, although he'd never seen proof of that. Thor and Tryg had met him during the day that first time, and they hadn't shown any hints that they were uncomfortable. They'd been wearing sunglasses, though, and Cecil was ready to bet they'd slathered their skin with sunscreen before leaving their hotel even though the day had been cloudy.

He stretched his arms, his hand tangling in a blanket he didn't remember using. Had Thor put it on him when he came back from grocery shopping? It was the only thing that made sense, and Cecil's heart felt like it went a bit soft. Cecil wasn't used to people taking care of him. Even the person he considered his best friend, Mabel, didn't spend enough time with him to do that. Cecil missed it, even though he'd never really had someone take care of him. His mother hadn't been the motherly type, and they'd never been close, which was why he'd been surprised when she left her powers to him. He'd been alone ever since he was a teenager, and he'd been okay with that. He still was, mostly. But he was discovering there was more to life than he'd imagined, and he wasn't sure how he'd deal with things once he was safe and Thor went back to his own life.

Of course, that was if he made it out of the situation alive. No one could promise him that would happen, and he didn't want to lie to himself. He had to face the facts — Fabrice was much more powerful than he was, and he was used to using the powers he'd stolen to hurt people. Nothing would stop him from trying to get the powers he thought Cecil had stolen from him, even though he didn't need them.

Cecil folded the blanket and put it back on the couch. Whatever the reasons behind Thor's behavior, he knew Thor wasn't going to change his mind about protecting him. He didn't want to think about that right now, though. It was too easy to obsess over how Fabrice could hurt Thor if Thor tried to step between Fabrice and Cecil. He was already thinking about it too often, considering he couldn't do anything to stop Thor. He'd tried, and he probably should try again, but he needed a few days to put together his thoughts and plan. Leaving everything behind and going out there without having a plan would be the worst thing that could happen. It would make him even more vulnerable when it came to

Fabrice. And even though Cecil knew Fabrice was more powerful, he wasn't going to make it easy for his brother to grab him and kill him.

He blinked when he stepped into the bright kitchen. He'd known Thor was cooking from the smell, but he hadn't expected the sight that greeted him. Thor had his back to Cecil and was focused on the stove. He was barefoot and wearing an apron, and he was shaking his hips and his head to the sound of the music that came from his phone on the counter next to him. He looked relaxed, as if he wasn't protecting Cecil from his crazy brother, and Cecil didn't want to interrupt him.

Thor turned around before Cecil could go back to the living room, though. He was holding a wooden spoon to his mouth as if it were a microphone, and he sang into it even after he noticed Cecil standing there. He wasn't ashamed of the situation Cecil had caught him in, and Cecil couldn't help but relax.

He smiled, powerless not to. "The God of thunder singing in his kitchen. I never imagined I'd be in this kind of situation."

Thor narrowed his eyes. "I already told you, I'm not the God of thunder. I'm much more good-looking than that actor."

Cecil couldn't deny that. They were both blond and handsome and *golden*, but Thor — *Cecil's* Thor — had an edge to him. Cecil wasn't sure what it was, but he suspected it had to do with Thor's piercings. Cecil had always liked piercings, although not on himself. He thought he was too soft to have them, but Thor didn't have that problem. The piercings made him more handsome. They made something churn low in his stomach, but he wasn't ready to examine that feeling right now.

Cecil cleared his throat. "Do you need help?"

"Depends. Are you going to sing and dance with me?"

Cecil felt his cheeks heat. "I don't dance. Or sing. Trust me. You don't want me to sing."

Thor grimaced. "That bad?"

"Probably worse than you can imagine. I can help with the food, though."

Thor turned back to the stove. "There's not much left to do. The water is boiling, so I'm going to dump the pasta in after I salt it. You could stir the sauce, but there's not much space at the stove, so you might as well just set the table."

Cecil was okay with that. He might have offered to help cook, but he was slightly afraid he'd poison them if he tried. Thor looked like he knew what he was doing, so Cecil felt okay with letting him take care of that.

It took him a few attempts to find the plates, glasses, and napkins in the cupboards. The silverware was easy, since it was in the first drawer, and the table was set by the time the pasta was cooked. Cecil sat at the table, briefly closing his eyes as he took in the delicious scent of the steaming plate of pasta in front of him. If the smell was the anything to go by, Thor was a good cook, and Cecil couldn't wait to fill his stomach.

"Dig in," Thor said, pointing his fork at Cecil's plate.

They were both silent for some time and focused on the food. It was as good as Cecil had hoped, and he ate way too much. He started to slow down after the first few forkfuls, and he tried it to enjoy everything that came with the meal. "This is nice."

Thor smiled. "You were worried I couldn't cook?"

"Well, a bit, but that wasn't what I was talking about. I meant that it's nice not to eat alone, and to eat food that has been prepared especially for you by someone who knows you. It's like a home cooked meal, and I don't often have those."

"You can't cook?"

"Not really, and that means I survive on microwave meals

and takeout."

Thor grimaced. "Those aren't good for you."

Thor wasn't being hunted by his brother, but Cecil didn't say it out loud. "I know. But trust me, microwave meals are better than my cooking. I'd have been dead a long time already if I had to eat my food."

"I'm sure you're exaggerating."

"Trust me. I'm not. I can show you sometime, if you want."

The corner of Thor's lips curled. "I look forward to it."

They both ignored the fact this might be one of the few meals they'd have together. Cecil didn't have the power to see the future, and on days like this one, he wished he did. He knew seeing the future was an unreliable power, but it would be better than wondering how long he still had to live.

Cecil wanted to live for a long time. He needed to find out would happen between him and Thor. He could tell there was something there, something that would grow if it had the chance to. Now he just needed to give it that chance.

CHAPTER EIGHT

Thor knew things were bad when Tryg called him at six the next morning. They'd been planning to talk, but Thor knew Tryg had better things to do at six AM. That meant something had happened, and Thor wasn't looking forward to finding out what that something was.

He dried his face and hands with a towel, then grabbed his phone. "What's wrong?"

Tryg huffed out a laugh. "Why do you think something is wrong?"

"That's the only reason you have to call me at this time of the morning."

"Did I wake you up?"

"Nope. I was training." Thor hadn't been able to sleep well last night. He kept thinking about Cecil and what would happen to him if Fabrice got close enough.

He needed details on what Fabrice could do. Cecil had been hesitant to give them to him, and honestly, Thor didn't blame him. Who would want to talk about all the ways your brother could kill you if he got his hands on you? Cecil was safe, but they both knew it was only temporary. No matter how hard Thor would try to keep Cecil safe, there was always a chance Fabrice would find him and take what he wanted from him.

Thor swallowed. "What happened?" He needed to know if he had to grab Cecil and run.

Tryg sighed. "Fabrice found out Cecil was in Brussels. I don't know how, but he's been tearing through the supernatural community in the city. He's trying to find someone who can tell him where Cecil is."

"And has he found someone?"

"Of course not. Only the three of us know where Cecil is. But Fabrice is trying, and something is bound to break sooner or later. When I said he was tearing through the community, I meant that literally. There were casualties."

Thor swore. Cecil was going to hate that when he found out. He didn't want anyone to get hurt because of him, and Thor knew he was going to blame himself for it. It wasn't his fault, but Cecil wouldn't see it like that. He'd blame himself, and if Thor knew him, he'd try to do something stupid sooner or later. Thor would have to look out for it. He wouldn't allow anyone to put Cecil in danger, not even Cecil.

"He's powerful, Thor," Tryg said.

Thor could hear the worry in Tryg's voice. He shared it. He needed to have a chat with Cecil about Fabrice, but he wasn't looking forward to it. He'd have to explain to Cecil what had happened, and hopefully, Cecil would allow him to support him through it. Thor wasn't sure he would, though. Cecil was so used to being alone that sometimes it looked like he didn't know how to let people in. Thor knew he was very much the same, but he had Tryg, and that helped. He wanted to be that person for Cecil. He wanted to be Cecil's Tryg or something like that.

Thor cleared his throat. "How powerful?"

"He killed four people."

"That only means he's ruthless."

"He used his magic. He didn't even touch those people, as far as I could find out."

That was worrying. Thor didn't have a clue how they were going to deal with Fabrice, but he was going to find a way. He had to. "We have magic, too."

"We do, but not like this. Not this kind of magic. I don't

know how Fabrice became so powerful, but we need to find out. We can't take him on if we don't know."

"I'll talk to Cecil."

"You do that. I'm keeping Isaac home right now."

Thor didn't ask where Tryg and Isaac were. He didn't need to know, and Tryg wouldn't tell him anyway. "You're still going to look into this?"

"Of course I am. I told you I'd help, and I'm going to do it. I know Cecil is important to you, even though I don't understand how it happened."

"How did Isaac become important to you?"

"You have a point. I'm going to try to find out where Fabrice is headed now that he knows Cecil isn't in Brussels. I can't make any promises, but I'll contact you if I find anything else. I wouldn't worry too much about Fabrice right now. He has no way to find out where Cecil is, and even if he does, you're with Cecil."

"You think I can beat him in a fight?"

"I don't know. I'd like to think the answer to that is yes, but we have no idea what we're up against."

"We're draugr. We're powerful enough."

"We're more powerful than a lot of the paranormal creatures we know about. That doesn't mean no one can beat us."

He was right. Thor was confident about what he could do—not only the powers he'd gained when he became a draugr, but also the training he'd been sure to maintain. But without knowing what kind of power Fabrice had, it was hard to plan a way to get around them.

"Let me know," he told Tryg.

"Will do. Keep Cecil safe. Isaac and I owe him everything."

Thor would have kept Cecil safe even if Cecil hadn't given Isaac immortality, but then, he'd never have met Cecil if Isaac and Tryg hadn't been looking for a mage to make that happen. The circumstances had played to their advantage.

Thor had a hard time focusing on his training after Tryg hung up. He kept imagining Fabrice capturing Cecil, and that was enough to tell him he was too close. He'd never cared about anyone when he'd been working in the past. Even before he'd taken on the task of being the handler for Tryg and the other killers he worked with, nothing had felt as personal as Cecil's case was. Of course, this wasn't exactly a case. It was nothing like what Thor had been used to. He had to kill someone, but no one was paying him to do it, and that was without considering the fact that he cared for Cecil more than he'd cared for anyone in a long time. He wasn't a protector, not usually. He wasn't sure where to start when it came to making sure nothing happened to Cecil.

He heard footsteps before he saw Cecil. He'd been going through his exercises without thinking about what he was doing, the routine both soothing and still insufficient to keep him from obsessing over what was happening. He'd shown the apartment to Cecil after dinner last night, so he wasn't surprised that after roaming through the living room and kitchen, Cecil headed toward the small guest room Thor had transformed into a gym.

Cecil appeared at the open door, and Thor's heart stuttered. Cecil was adorable. He was still sleep-rumpled, with creases on his cheek and his hair all over the place. He blinked at the harsh light in the gym and rubbed his eyes. "What's going on?"

"Nothing," Thor answered. He could hear how rough his voice was, and he cleared his throat. "I didn't expect you to wake up this early."

"I think I slept too much yesterday afternoon. I had a hard time falling asleep last night, and I'm not sleepy anymore."

Thor licked his lips. "Give me the time to shower, and we can have breakfast."

"I didn't come here to interrupt. I was just wondering

where you were. Feel free to finish training, or whatever you were doing."

Thor wasn't sure he could do that, not with Cecil staring at him the way he was and looking the way he looked.

Cecil wasn't going to drool. Oh God, he wasn't *already* drooling, was he?

He covertly raised his hand to his face and made sure of it, then rubbed his eye because he was almost sure this was a dream — and a good one, at that. He hadn't expected to stumble upon Thor being all glistening and panting and looking like he wouldn't budge if Cecil climbed him like a tree. Now that Cecil was more fully awake, there was no ignoring all that or denying that his morning wood was getting worse, not better. Cecil should have taken care of it earlier, but he'd barely had the mental capacity to remember to brush his teeth after washing his face. He hoped Thor wouldn't notice the bulge in his pants, but knowing his luck, Thor would and would get embarrassed and everything, and the situation would become a disaster.

Cecil should go back to bed, or at the very least, he should go back to his bedroom to take a cold shower.

He cleared his throat. "Right. I'm going to go. We can talk over breakfast."

He turned to leave, but he was balance challenged on his best of days, and this wasn't one of them — which didn't bode well, since he'd barely woken up. He was also still half asleep, half focused on the wonder that was a sweaty Thor, so of course, he managed to trip on the foot of one of the machines Thor had in his homemade gym. He tilted forward, and he knew it was going to hurt even if he managed to put his hands up to protect his face. He'd fallen on his face too many times not to know it was better to hurt his hands than his nose.

He never touched the floor. A strong arm wrapped around his waist from behind and hauled him back up. Cecil's back bumped against Thor's chest, and he sucked in a breath.

He felt safe. No matter how sexy Thor was, how good he smelled, that wasn't the most important thing. Cecil couldn't remember the last time he hadn't been afraid Fabrice would find him, the last time he'd been able to relax and forget about his brother. He still couldn't, but for the first time, he thought he might have a chance. Thor wasn't going to leave him alone. He was going to protect him, and hopefully, he'd be the reason Fabrice finally left Cecil alone.

Thor's arm loosened. "I'm sorry," he said, stepping back.

Cecil frowned and turned to look at him. "What for? You just saved my face from meeting the floor."

Thor grinned. "For sweating all over you."

Cecil had barely noticed it, but if he had, he knew he wouldn't have minded. A sweaty Thor was the thing Cecil's dreams were made of lately.

He licked his lips. "I don't mind."

Thor cocked his head. "Don't you?"

"No." Was that too revealing? The last thing Cecil wanted was to embarrass Thor by drooling all over him, or even making his crush obvious.

He swallowed and stepped back, but to his surprise, Thor moved with him, coming closer. Cecil tripped again, and Thor grabbed his forearms, guiding him until his back hit the closest wall.

Cecil licked his lips. He had no idea what was happening, but he was glad he'd already brushed his teeth. "What are you doing?" he asked, his voice little more than a croak.

"You said you didn't mind if I got you sweaty."

And didn't *that* make images pop into Cecil's mind! Images he probably shouldn't think too much about if he didn't want Thor to notice that the soft pants that he'd slept in were tenting. "I don't."

"Why not? It's sweat. You're not supposed to like it, not unless it's in a particular situation."

For fuck's sake. There was no way this was innocent. Cecil didn't know if Thor had noticed his crush or if he shared it, but at this point, he needed to know. They were going to be around each other for a while, so it might make things painfully awkward, but Cecil didn't think so.

Or he hoped it wouldn't.

He reached forward with a trembling hand and pressed it against Thor's chest. Thor's t-shirt felt damp and molded to his chest, and Cecil couldn't help himself — he moved his fingers until he reached Thor's nipple and circled it. It puckered, exposing the piercing in it even more. Not that Cecil had needed to do that to notice the piercing, but damn.

"What are you doing?" Thor asked in a murmur. He wrapped his fingers around Cecil's wrist, but he didn't push him away, and Cecil hoped that was another sign that Thor wanted this as much as he did.

"What I've wanted to do since basically the moment I first saw you."

Thor breath hitched. "Have you?"

Cecil didn't look at him. He couldn't. It was easier to focus on the piercing, and he moved his fingers to the other nipple to outline the second piercing there. "Yes."

"Good." There was a growl in Thor's voice now, and Cecil snapped his head up in surprise.

He didn't have the time to say anything, not before Thor took him into his arms and mashed their lips together.

It took Cecil a moment to get over his shock and answer the kiss. He clutched Thor's forearms and tried to get himself closer to him as he opened his mouth, almost laughing in relief and happiness when Thor pressed him against the wall until there wasn't an inch of space between their bodies.

Thor reached down to cup Cecil's ass, and when he did, Cecil hopped up and wrapped his legs around Thor's waist. He didn't even stop to think that maybe Thor wouldn't be able to hold his weight up. Thor stumbled slightly, but that was it. He continued pushing Cecil against the wall, which no doubt helped him bear the weight — not that Cecil cared. As long as he didn't fall on his ass, he'd be okay.

Then Thor reached between them and pushed down Cecil's pajama pants, and Cecil realized he'd be *more* than okay.

He scrambled to do the same to Thor, wanting to see and feel more of his skin. He didn't know if this was just their first time or if it would be their only time, and he wasn't going to risk not ever touching Thor the way he'd been dreaming of.

"This won't work," he mumbled. He'd have to move back on the floor if he wanted to get rid of their pants, damn it.

Thor shook his head and batted Cecil's hands away. Cecil wasn't sure what he did or how he managed it, but his pants were suddenly hooked under his balls, and Thor's cock was rubbing against his, naked and pink and *glorious*. And if felt so fucking good against Cecil.

Thor bit Cecil's neck, making him shudder in pleasure and focus his attention back on Thor's face. "Kiss me," Thor murmured. At the same time, he wrapped his hand around both their cocks — and how the fuck did he manage to do that — and rubbed his thumb over the heads.

Cecil wasn't sure what happened after that. His body felt like it was burning with need as he kissed Thor and kept on kissing him while Thor worked both their cocks until Cecil felt like he was about to explode. He didn't want this to end, just in case it wouldn't happen again, but he could tell he wasn't going to last much longer, especially when he caught sight of Thor looking utterly fucked, with his hair messed up by Cecil's hands and his lips red and slick with Cecil's saliva.

Cecil groaned and hit the back of his head against the wall. It hurt, but it helped not to focus on his cock, at least until Thor added a twist to his hand on the upward movement.

"You're going to kill me," Cecil muttered as he brought his attention back to Thor. He kissed Thor again, even though Thor was chuckling into his mouth.

"That's not the point, not unless you die of pleasure, although I'd rather avoid that," Thor answered.

"Yeah?"

"Yeah. I'd like to do this again, so I'd rather keep you alive."

"You should make me come, then, because I feel like I'm gonna explode if you don't." Thor wanted to do this again. He wanted a repeat of this slice of heaven on earth, and Cecil was all for it.

He dug his nails into Thor's shoulders and panted into Thor's mouth, screwing his eyes shut when he couldn't resist anymore. He was going to come whether he liked it or not — and he very much liked it right now — so he let go, tensing and then slumping against Thor's chest as he came between them and got both their t-shirts dirty.

Thor didn't seem to care, because he added his cum to Cecil's with a grunt and a few more movements of his hand. Then they stood there, wrapped around each other, panting in unison, and on Cecil's part, with no idea what to do.

CHAPTER NINE

Thor wasn't sorry about what had just happened, but he wasn't sure how to handle it.

He didn't usually have that kind of problem after sex, but that was mostly because he never hung around for long once he came. He couldn't exactly leave Cecil alone in the apartment, though. Besides, he didn't want to leave Cecil on his own. For the first time in years, Thor wanted more than sex. He wasn't quite sure how to go with that, so he kept his mouth shut as he set Cecil down. He held on, since Cecil's knees seemed not to be working well, and he tried his hardest not to feel smug about that.

Cecil reached down to smooth his t-shirt and grimaced when he touched the semen they'd both left there. "We should probably wash up," he said.

Thor agreed. He'd already been sweaty because he'd been training, and now he felt even dirtier, albeit in a good way. He'd sweated even more while having sex with Cecil, and he felt sticky. It wasn't the greatest feeling, and he couldn't wait to shower. He still hesitated, unsure if Cecil had meant they should shower together. One of them had to move, though, so he took a step back.

Cecil's cheeks were flushed, and it was a good look on him. Thor wanted to see it happening more often, but he realized how strange the situation was. He didn't want to crowd Cecil, and that was precisely what he was going to do if he didn't start moving.

He rubbed the back of his neck. "I'll see you for breakfast?"

Thor couldn't tell if his suggestion hurt Cecil. Cecil wasn't looking at him, so he headed out, relieved when Cecil came right after him, gently touching the small of his back as they separated to go to their respective bedrooms. It wasn't the conversation they needed to have, but it made Thor feel better about the situation.

He was in the kitchen, having already started cooking breakfast, when Cecil arrived. He was wearing a pair of jeans and a t-shirt, tighter this time. Thor couldn't help but stare, smiling when Cecil's cheeks reddened. He didn't want Cecil to feel awkward, but he doubted anything he could do or say would help with that. They needed to talk, but hopefully, it could wait until after breakfast. Thor was ravenous.

Cecil flopped into one of the chairs and filled a mug with coffee. He took a sip, and Thor heard him sigh from where he was at the stove. Thor filled two plates with eggs and bacon and brought them to the table. Cecil smiled in thanks, and they both settled down to eat.

Things still felt awkward between them. Thor wasn't sure what to do to make it stop, and he suspected his best option would be to keep his mouth shut. He wasn't great with words, and even less with cute men that he'd just had sex with. He couldn't help but notice the way Cecil was pushing his eggs around the plate with his fork. He didn't look very interested in the food, and Thor wasn't sure why that was.

He should tell Cecil about his brother. He should have done so earlier before they'd had sex, but the occasion hadn't presented itself, and Thor didn't think interrupting what they'd been doing would have been a good idea. Cecil would have probably nailed his ass to the wall for not making him come or something.

The clang of Cecil's fork on his plate made Thor look up. "Are we going to talk about it?" Cecil asked.

Thor blinked. Was Cecil reading his mind? "I agree."

Cecil looked nonplussed. "Really?"

Thor put his fork down. "I should have told you earlier. Tryg called me. Your brother—"

Cecil reached for Thor. Thor stopped talking, his eyes widening when Cecil slapped him on the back of the head. Cecil moved back as Thor rubbed the spot he'd just hit.

"What was that for?" Thor asked.

"That's not what I meant when I said we should talk."

"You didn't have to hit me for that."

Cecil stuffed a bit of bacon into his mouth. "I didn't hit you hard. Stop exaggerating things."

"You need to know what your brother is up to."

"And I'll find out soon enough. I don't want to ruin breakfast talking about it."

"But you want to talk about what just happened in the gym."

"Unless you're going to tell me it was a mistake and that it will never happen again. That would ruin breakfast even more than what Fabrice is up to."

Thor didn't think that was true, but he wasn't going to push, not when Cecil looked relaxed for the first time since Thor had met him. "We had sex," he said instead.

Cecil was adorable with a blush on his face. "I noticed."

"Why should we talk about it?" Thor asked, even though he knew why they should.

"What did it mean? Are we going to do it again? Or are you going to tell me to fuck off?"

"Never. I already told you, I'm here to stay, at least until your brother has been dealt with."

"And after that?"

Thor wasn't sure how to answer that question. He wanted to tell Cecil they were meant to be together, and maybe they were. But they were both used to being on their own. Would they be able to deal with suddenly having someone else in their lives? Could they learn to be together as a couple? Should they even do that right now? Cecil was terrified. He thought his brother was going to kill him, and he wasn't wrong. Fabrice would if he ever got his hands on Cecil.

But Thor didn't want Cecil to be with him just because he needed a protector. It might not have bothered him with anyone else, but it did with Cecil, and that told Thor that Cecil had become important to him. He didn't know how that had happened, or why, but the how and why didn't matter.

"You're starting to freak me out," Cecil said.

That was the last thing Thor wanted. "I'm sorry. I'm just not sure how to answer that."

"Tell me what you want. That's all."

Thor sucked in a breath. "I want to try. I don't know what's going on between us, if it's because of the situation we're in or because we like each other, but I want to see where things go. Most of all, I don't want to force myself not to touch you or kiss you, when we both want it. I don't want to make myself resist being with you, not when there isn't a good reason."

Cecil snorted. "Most people would say that having a homicidal half brother trying to get to me is a good enough reason not to want to start anything."

Thor reached over the table and grabbed one of Cecil's hands. He squeezed it, trying to convey how he felt without saying it. He wasn't sure Cecil got it, though, so he added, "I'm not most people. You should know that by now."

"Trust me. I'm aware of that."

"I'm staying with you, Cecil. I don't care about your brother, at least not beyond trying to protect you from him. We'll deal with him together, and once that's done, we'll be able to focus on each other."

"And in the meantime, we can have sex?"

Thor burst out laughing. "Yes, we can have sex. I told you, I think there could be something between us, and I want to see where it goes. I can't promise forever, because I don't think we know each other well enough for that, not yet, but I want to see if the possibility of forever is there."

The thought terrified Thor. He didn't get forever with others. He'd thought he'd have to watch Tryg and Isaac be happy from the sidelines, but now he had a possibility of having that himself, and he wasn't sure how to deal with it. He and Cecil weren't in a hurry, but they couldn't ignore the danger Fabrice represented. They wouldn't have anything if they didn't take care of him, and while Thor had been convinced before, he was even more so now.

Cecil needed to tell Thor precisely what he was going to face once Fabrice found them. He'd never forgive himself for not telling Thor everything and causing his death or any kind of wounds Fabrice might inflict.

"You should know about Fabrice."

Thor wrinkled his nose. "You already told me about him."

"I didn't tell you everything, though. I should have, considering the situation—but everything was a mess, and I was afraid you'd run the other way."

"You're not afraid of that happening anymore?"

"I am, but I realize I have to trust you. I don't have an alternative, and I *want* to trust you." Cecil couldn't remember the last time he'd wanted something so much.

Thor squeezed Cecil's hand again. "Tell me."

Cecil sighed. "I told you Fabrice wants my mother's power. The only way for him to get it is if I decide to give it to him."

"Something you said you'd never do."

"I want to think I'd never do it, but Fabrice has been stealing powers for decades. He knows what to do or say for people to give them up, and then he kills them."

"How does he convince people? How many times has he

done it?"

Cecil shook his head. "I don't know how many people he's killed over the years. He tortures them until they give him their power, then he kills them." That was part of what scared Cecil so much. He didn't think he would be this afraid if Fabrice only wanted to kill him. He wasn't suicidal, but he'd been running for so long — too long. He was tired. He was terrified of what Fabrice would do if he got to him more than he was afraid of death, though.

"So he could have powers we don't know about."

"Exactly. What were you going to say before I slapped you?"

Thor cleared his throat. "Tryg called me earlier, before you got to the gym. He told me your brother has been tearing through Brussels trying to find you. He killed people, Cecil."

Cecil's stomach dropped, and he felt like he was going to throw up. He'd known Fabrice wouldn't stop for anything to get to him. He'd been so focused on saving himself and Thor that he'd barely spared a thought for the people Fabrice was hurting. "How many?"

"Four."

Cecil was grateful Thor didn't try to convince him this wasn't his fault. Logically, he knew it wasn't. He wasn't the one who'd killed those people. He hadn't even been in the same city as them. His brother was the killer, and those weren't the only four people he'd killed. Even if Cecil ignored the people Fabrice had killed for their powers, he knew how cruel his brother was. Fabrice killed because he enjoyed it — because he wanted to. Even if Cecil had surrendered to him, even if he'd managed to get Fabrice to promise he wouldn't hurt anyone else, he knew Fabrice would have lied. He probably would have hurt someone in front of Cecil just because he could, and because he knew how much it would hurt Cecil.

Cecil swallowed. "Is there anything I can do for the

victims' families?"

"I don't know. I'll ask Tryg to look into it, if you want me to."

Cecil nodded. "Please. I want to help. I couldn't do anything to save their loved ones, and whatever I do now isn't going to be enough or to bring them back, but hopefully, it will help at least a bit."

"We'll stop him."

Thor looked so convinced that Cecil almost believed him. He wanted to believe him, but he'd been fighting with his brother for so long that he didn't dare to. "He has powers we can't even imagine."

"Is there any way for us to find out what they are?"

Cecil bit his lower lip. He didn't want to do this, and he avoided it until now, but he thought it was time. "I can dream-walk."

Thor blinked. "So can I."

"What I meant is, I can dream-walk into Fabrice's dreams. I'm not sure I'll be able to find out what he can do like that, but I can't think of anything else right now."

"It's too dangerous. You have no idea what your brother will do to you if he catches you."

"Maybe not, but I can't just wait and see what happens next, not when Fabrice is killing people to find me."

"Getting yourself killed isn't going to help, either."

Maybe not, but at least, if Cecil was dead, Fabrice would stop hunting him across Europe. "Do you have a better idea?"

Thor rubbed his face. "Not right now, but give me a few hours and I'll come up with something."

"All right. But if you can't find anything else, I'll dream-walk tonight." Cecil wasn't going to back off from this. He'd run for too long, and he was done with that. He was going to stop Fabrice, whatever it took. He hoped he wasn't going to die before finding out what was between him and Thor, but he was ready to sacrifice that and so much more to make sure Fabrice couldn't hurt anyone else, ever.

Thor rose from his chair. "I'm going to call Tryg."

Cecil watched him walk out of the kitchen. He suspected Thor was angry, although probably not just with him. Cecil could imagine Thor was petrified, and he obviously wasn't used to that. From what Cecil had noticed, Thor wasn't quite sure how to deal with it, and he lashed out. It made sense. To be honest, Cecil wasn't sure how to get over the paralyzing fear, either, but he needed to think about the people his brother was hurting. He couldn't focus on himself and what he wanted, not right now, not until Fabrice wasn't a danger anymore.

He took his time cleaning up the kitchen. He wasn't sure what to do now. He had to wait until late tonight before he could dream-walk, and it left him an entire day with nothing to do except obsess over Fabrice and what he was doing. He flopped on the couch once he was done and took out his phone. He'd turned it off before doing Isaac's manipulation, and he hadn't turned it on again. Fabrice wouldn't be able to trace him through it—Cecil had made sure of that when he bought it—so he did so now. He wasn't surprised to see increasingly alarmed text messages from Mabel. She'd probably heard about what had happened in Brussels, about what Fabrice was doing. Cecil hadn't told her he was leaving Paris, but Paris was close to Brussels, close enough for her to worry about Fabrice finding him.

He quickly dialed her number and waited for her to answer.

"Cecil? Are you okay? Where are you? What happened?" Mabel asked as soon as she answered.

Cecil blinked at the onslaught of questions. "Slow down."

"Slow down? Are you serious? You disappeared for days, and I didn't worry, because you often do that. But when I found out Fabrice was in Brussels killing people, I started worrying. Did he find you?"

"He did. I don't know how he did it, but I had to run." Cecil didn't tell her about Brussels. She didn't need to be aware of what had happened.

"How did he know you were in Brussels?"

Cecil frowned. "How did *you* know?"

"That doesn't matter. Where are you now? Do you need me to come to you? Are you hurt?"

"I'm fine, Mabel. I promise. And no, I don't want you to come to me. I can't risk it."

"I hate the fact that you're alone facing this."

Cecil wasn't going to tell her about Thor. He didn't want to put Thor's life in danger. Telling Mabel was a risk he couldn't take, not when it came to Thor. "I'll be fine, I promise. I'm not in Belgium anymore, and I didn't go back to Paris."

"You're not going to tell me where you are?"

"I never do. What's going on, Mabel?"

"Apart from the fact that your brother almost got to you? Cecil, you have to see you can't go on like this forever. Fabrice is going to find you, and he's going to hurt you. I can't just stand back and let him do that."

"You're going to get hurt if you try to intervene. I won't allow that." No matter how little time he and Mabel spent together or how rarely they talked, she was still his friend. Enough people had already paid for something they had nothing to do with. Losing Mabel would break Cecil, so he wasn't going to allow that. "I'm fine. That's all you need to know. I'll call you again if anything changes, I promise." He hoped he'd have good news when he did, but he wasn't going to make any promises he wasn't sure he could keep.

Thor was worried. He couldn't deny he didn't want Cecil to

dream-walk. He knew he had no say into what Cecil did or didn't do, but it was hard to accept the possibility that Cecil might get hurt. He'd become important to Thor in such a short time, and Thor had no idea how to deal with that. He just wasn't used to caring so much about people who weren't Tryg, and he knew Tryg could take care of himself. Cecil probably could, too, but Thor didn't know if that was really true. He didn't know Cecil, and this situation was showing him exactly how little he did.

He couldn't veto this, though. He was tempted to, but it wasn't like he and Cecil were a couple, even though they'd had sex that morning. Thor had no say in Cecil's life beyond trying to protect him, and even though Cecil could be hurt in this situation, Thor just couldn't force him into anything. He was terrified, but since he couldn't change Cecil's mind, he would support him through the dream-walk.

At least he knew what this was about. Draugr had that ability as well, although Thor suspected it wasn't quite the same as Cecil's. He was going to ask Cecil a lot of questions before allowing him to do anything, though. There was no way he was going into this blind, whatever Cecil thought or felt.

"You look like you're about to punch a hole in the wall."

Thor glared at Cecil. "Shut it."

Cecil arched a brow. "I just want to know if the walls will be safe while I'm doing this."

"I'm not going to hurt the walls. And you're not doing anything until you explain exactly what you're going to do and what's supposed to happen."

Cecil was sitting cross-legged on the bed in the guest room. He was wearing soft, comfortable clothes that Thor kind of wanted to tear off his body. The corner of it is lips curled into a half-smile. "Why am I not surprised?"

"Because you already know me well enough to be aware of the fact that I won't let you put yourself in danger if I can't help keeping you safe."

Cecil's expression softened. "I'll be fine. You told me you know what dream-walking is like, right?"

Thor nodded.

"Then you know how it works," Cecil continued. "I'm just going to find Fabrice and walk into his dreams. I'm going to try to talk to him and convince him to leave me alone. That's all."

Thor crossed his harm over his chest. "He could hurt you."

"No, he can't. I'll be right here on the bed. He can't do anything to me, not in our dreams. That's kind of the point."

"Hags can hurt people through their dreams."

Cecil scowled. "Only the people they're sitting on while dream-walking. I'm not going to be anywhere near close to Fabrice. He can't do anything to me in the dream world."

Thor wanted to be as convinced of that as Cecil was. "You said yourself that you don't know what kind of power he harvested from the people he killed. As far as I know, he could have managed to find someone who can hurt other people in their dreams. You have no way to know, or no way to defend yourself if that's the case."

Cecil sighed. "You're right. I have no way of knowing that. I have to do something, and this is the only safe thing I can think of. I'm all ears if you have another option, though."

Thor scowled. Cecil knew damn well that he didn't have suggestions. He'd have told him already if he had. "Why haven't you already done this, if it's as easy as you make it sound?"

Cecil's cheeks reddened. "I've been running most of my life. I never thought I'd have a chance against Fabrice. I still don't think I do, especially considering everything. But I'm going to try. I'm done running, and I'm facing him."

Thor felt like this new assertive Cecil was there because of him. He'd be happy in any other situation. He wanted Cecil to live his life fighting for what he wanted instead of spending his time running and being afraid. But this assertive Cecil was also the one who was putting himself in danger, and Thor was less okay with that. "He's not going to listen to you."

Thor knew Cecil hoped to change his brother's mind about taking away his power as painfully as he could. Thor didn't have to have met Fabrice to know that wasn't going to happen. Fabrice was bent on hurting Cecil, and nothing would stop him from doing just that, especially nothing Cecil could say to him. It wasn't a question of powers, not anymore. It was the question of revenge and bitterness. There was nothing Cecil could do against that.

Thor suspected Cecil was going to attempt to push Fabrice's affection button. He was going to talk about their mother, and maybe about their earlier relationship. Thor didn't think Fabrice had always been a homicidal maniac. Even if he and Cecil had never been close, they'd no doubt been closer than they were now — which wasn't difficult, since Fabrice was actively trying to kill his brother. Cecil was going to try to pull on their old relationship, and it wasn't going to work.

From what Thor had seen and gathered, the only reason Fabrice had to live was Fabrice. Nothing and no one would change that, and if Thor was right, Fabrice was going to be pissed about having his brother walking around his dreams. That would make him even angrier and push him into trying even harder to get to Cecil.

But Thor was going to be there. He would make sure Cecil was okay. He didn't like dream-walking, just like he didn't like reading the future, but he'd do both if that was what was he needed to keep the man he was starting to care too much about safe.

CHAPTER TEN

Cecil had never done this. He'd dream-walked before, of course, but never in his brother's mind. He didn't know what he'd find there. He wasn't sure he wanted to find out, but he was about to. At least Thor would be there, waiting for him when he woke up again, protecting his body from any harm that might come to him while he was unconscious. Having the presence there helped more than Cecil would have thought. He didn't know if it was because it was Thor, or because he wouldn't be alone, but the *why* didn't matter.

He wasn't as convinced as he'd tried to show to Thor. He knew Fabrice was going to be angry when he realized what was happening. He would do everything in his power to kick Cecil out of his dreams and his mind, and Cecil needed to work around that. He'd have to resist his brother for as long as he needed to talk to him.

Cecil wasn't an idiot. He wasn't delusional. He knew Fabrice probably wouldn't listen to him. He was going in fully aware of that, but that didn't change the fact that he wanted to try. Thor wanted to kill Fabrice without asking questions, and Cecil could admit things would probably end that way whatever he did to avoid it. But he'd never be able to forgive himself if he didn't at least *try*.

Fabrice deserved a chance to explain what he was doing and why. He deserved a chance to change his mind, if that was what he wanted. Cecil doubted that would happen, but he would try anyway.

He was on his bed, stretched out on his back. He'd already

taken the herbs that were supposed to help him sleep. Things would be different if he could somehow get into Fabrice's bedroom, but since he didn't know where Fabrice was and he didn't want to put himself in danger that way, this would have to do.

"I'm not going anywhere," Thor murmured from the corner of the bedroom where he was standing.

Knowing he was there helped, and Cecil closed his eyes and tried to relax. The sooner he fell asleep, the sooner he'd be in Fabrice's dreams and sooner he could come out of them.

He wasn't sure how much time had passed, but he knew the moment he was asleep.

He opened his eyes, and he wasn't in the bedroom anymore. He wasn't *inside* anymore. He couldn't see much apart from what seemed to be a thick fog, but this wasn't the first time he'd dream-walked, so he'd expected this. It was the place where he always started when he did this. Now he had to find Fabrice and get to him. It wasn't going to be easy. There was no way Fabrice wasn't aware of the fact that Cecil could do this. If he was smart — and he was — he'd make sure no one could enter his mind while he was sleeping every night.

Since they were related, Cecil didn't have too much of a problem finding Fabrice's mind. He followed the bond they shared even though neither of them wanted it. The fog moved around Cecil, letting him pass before it closed back again behind him. It felt claustrophobic, and Cecil had to push down the slight panic bubbling in his chest.

He could do this. Fabrice wouldn't be able to hurt him, not in their dreams. He was safe, no matter how afraid he was.

He realized he'd arrived when he had to stop. He was in front of Fabrice's mind, but he couldn't move forward. An invisible force field was stopping him from taking even one step ahead. He needed to find a way around it or through it.

He wrinkled his nose and poked at the field. It felt elastic, but it didn't give, no matter how hard he pushed. He couldn't get his finger through it.

Fabrice couldn't dream-walk. Like the manipulation of death, it was a power Cecil had gotten from their mother. Fabrice might have been able to steal dream-walking from someone else, but Cecil doubted he'd bothered. He didn't understand that dreams and dream-walking could be as powerful and useful as the other powers he had. He'd protected his mind, but that was it.

That meant Cecil was stronger than him, at least in their minds. He could poke a hole in the shield and slip in, and Fabrice wouldn't realize it until Cecil was standing in front of him.

It took a bit of effort for Cecil to get through the shield. He was doing his best to keep Fabrice from noticing, so he had to be careful, quiet, and gentle.

The world was different in Fabrice's mind.

It looked like a palace, with marble and gold everywhere. It wasn't to Cecil's taste, but he had expected nothing different. That was exactly what Fabrice felt like to him. Full of himself and convinced he deserved all the best things in life. Cecil was ready to bet that the palace's foundation was crumbling and rotting, very much like the foundation of Fabrice's personality. Fabrice wasn't a good man, no matter how pretty he was. The same went for his mind. It looked okay from the first look, although it was anything but.

Now Cecil had to find his brother.

He suspected he'd find Fabrice in the heart of the building. He'd be able to control everything from there, to survey his kingdom.

Cecil was right. He found Fabrice where he'd thought he would, in a huge bedroom, sitting on a chair by the window.

He didn't turn around when Cecil still stepped in, but Cecil knew his brother was aware he wasn't alone anymore.

Neither of them talked for a few seconds. Cecil hesitated, then decided he might as well be the first one to speak. "Fabrice."

"I expected you sooner." Fabrice didn't even bother turning to look at Cecil. Cecil wasn't offended. He wasn't sure he wanted to face his brother.

"I was hoping I wouldn't have to come by."

"You shouldn't have bothered. This isn't going to change anything."

Cecil had known that, but his chest still felt like it crumbled under the weight of disappointment. "Why are you doing this? I know that you've been hunting powers all over the world in the past decades. You don't need mine."

Fabrice finally turned. He looked like he had when they'd been younger. Cecil didn't know if that was the way Fabrice saw himself or if he still looked like this. "Manipulating death isn't a power everyone has."

"You don't need it. You're already immortal."

"I might not need it, but I want it. It's mine, and I should be the one earning money through it, not you."

"I can stop using it." Cecil didn't like that thought, but he was ready to do this if it meant that Fabrice would stop coming after him.

Fabrice snorted. "Not using it isn't going to make a difference. You don't deserve that power. It should have been mine, and it's going to be soon enough."

"Our mother left it to me. I didn't make that decision."

"Even if you didn't, she should have left it to me. I deserved it."

Cecil swallowed. He hadn't expected to be able to change his brother's mind. He'd wanted to try, but just like he'd suspected, he was going to go back to Thor without results.

"It's unfair," Fabrice continued. "I was the eldest son. I was the one closest to our mother. Her powers belong to me. You were always too weak for them."

Cecil straightened. "I'm not too weak to use them."

"Not to use them, no, but are you using them the way you're supposed to?"

Cecil's thoughts drifted to Isaac. "Yes."

Fabrice snorted. "Of course you think so. You think helping people is what those powers were made for. You believe that crap about hags being protective spirits and whatever. But that wasn't what you were supposed to do with the powers. You have them. They make you so powerful and *better* than everyone else on earth. You should take advantage of that. You should crush people instead of helping them. You have the power to control them and make them do whatever you want, to earn as much money as you want. The fact that you aren't doing those things is the reason you shouldn't have those powers."

Cecil took a step back. There was no talking his brother out of this. Fabrice was too far gone. There would be no changing his mind, no matter how hard Cecil tried.

Fabrice rose from his chair and faced his brother. Cecil could tell he was going to try to attack him, but he didn't move. Fabrice couldn't hurt him, not in the dream world.

But when Fabrice moved toward Cecil, Cecil felt him. He felt Fabrice's hands on his neck. He felt Fabrice start squeezing.

Then he jerked awake.

Thor was there when Cecil snapped up into a sitting position. He'd known something was wrong when Cecil had started to get agitated. He hadn't intervened because he knew that waking up Cecil would be the worst thing he could do in this case.

It hadn't been easy to stay away, but he'd waited, at least until Cecil's distress had become more apparent and fingerprints had started forming on Cecil's throat. That had been enough for Thor to freak out.

Cecil's eyes were wide and afraid. He looked around frantically as if expecting someone to attack him. Thor didn't have to ask to know that was exactly what Fabrice had done. He didn't understand how Fabrice had managed, and right now, he didn't care. The one thing he cared about was Cecil.

He gently wrapped his fingers around Cecil's wrists to make sure Cecil didn't flail around and hurt himself. "You're okay. You're awake. He can't hurt you anymore. He's not even here."

Cecil was still agitated, but it seemed like Thor's words were calming him down, at least a bit. Thor took a chance and wrapped his arms around Cecil, pulling him against his chest. He rubbed Cecil's back and murmured stupid little soothing words. He was ready to do just about anything to make sure Cecil was all right, but he was glad no one was there to see him. He didn't usually have it in him to comfort and soothe. But if this was what Cecil needed, then it was what Cecil would get.

"What happened?" Thor asked once Cecil had stopped shaking.

"He hurt me."

"How?"

"I don't know. He wasn't supposed to be able to touch me."

Thor had known something was going to happen, but he didn't want to tell Cecil *I told you so*. It wasn't what Cecil needed right now, or ever. He'd been trying to do the right thing, and Thor couldn't blame him for that. He wouldn't be Cecil otherwise, and Thor wouldn't be already halfway in love with him.

Thor gently pushed Cecil away. Cecil had been crying, and

his cheeks were still wet. "Come on. Let's go to the bathroom. You can wash up while I make you some tea. Then we can talk about what happened and how it happened."

"I don't know how it happened. It shouldn't have been possible."

"I know that. Don't worry. I'm not expecting you to have an answer. But we do have to talk about what happened." He skimmed his fingertips over the forming bruises on Cecil's throat. "This isn't normal." And it had to hurt, even though Cecil hadn't mentioned it.

Cecil gave up trying to protest and slid off the bed. Thor watched him disappear into the bathroom before he got up himself and headed to the kitchen. He didn't like what was happening, and he had no clue how to take care of Cecil. Maybe he should talk to Tryg and ask for pointers, but he doubted Tryg was awake right now. Even if he was, he wouldn't take being interrupted kindly. No, it would have to wait until tomorrow. Besides, no matter how much Thor wanted to solve this problem, he didn't think there was anything he could do right now beyond comforting Cecil and making sure he was okay.

Cecil's tea was ready by the time Cecil arrived in the kitchen. Thor didn't want to push, but once Cecil had drunk down half his cup, he asked, "What happened?"

Cecil sighed. He wrapped both hands around the cup. "I don't know. We were talking, and everything was as I expected them to be. It was nothing different from the other times I've dream-walked. Then Fabrice jumped at me, and I didn't move, because usually, nothing would have happened at that point."

"But something *did* happen."

"Yeah. I don't know how he did it, but he managed to wrap his hands around my throat."

Thor couldn't look at the bruises there without feeling

angry. He knew that wasn't what Cecil needed, so he pushed the anger down and focused on Cecil's well-being. "He hurt you."

"He did, but that's not the important thing right now. Do you know of any power he could have stolen that would give him the ability to touch me in the dream world?"

"No, but I can ask around." Thor would do that even if Cecil didn't think it was necessary, but he was glad to see that Cecil did. That made Fabrice even more dangerous than they thought he was. "Do you think he'd have been able to follow you to the human world? If you hadn't woken up?"

Cecil shook his head. "Not without me there, but I think he would have eventually killed me. My throat hurts for real, and I don't understand how that's possible." He looked straight at Thor. "You're the one who woke me up?"

Thor shook his head. "I know better than to wake you up while you're dream-walking. I don't know what happened, but I did touch you when you started thrashing around."

"Maybe that was enough to jerk me awake. Whatever you did, thank you. I'm not sure I would have managed without that. I don't know if I would have had the state of mind to pull myself out of the dream world."

"You can't do it again." Thor knew he couldn't force Cecil to do or not to do something, but he was ready to try if Cecil insisted on putting himself in danger. He respected Cecil for what he'd tried to do, but there would be no convincing Fabrice to stop what he was doing.

Thor reached out and stroked Cecil's hand. "Why don't we go to bed?"

Cecil blinked. "You mean, together?"

"If you want to. I was thinking you might not want to be alone tonight."

"You're right. I don't. I just wasn't sure how to ask."

Thor got up and went to Cecil. He kissed the top of Cecil's

head and breathed in his scent. He'd come too close to losing him tonight, and he wouldn't allow that to happen ever again. "You never have to ask. Come on, let's go to bed."

There was nothing sexual in the way they cuddled together under the blanket. Cecil needed to feel close to someone and to feel safe, and that was what Thor was going to give him. They fell asleep like that, and Thor slept more deeply than he could remember sleeping in the past decades.

That was why the sound of his phone ringing was so startling.

He could tell it was bad news just from the fact that it was still dark outside. He didn't know what time it was, but he answered without checking. "Yes?"

"He's in Scotland."

Thor blinked. "What?"

"Fabrice. I don't know how he found you, but he's in Scotland."

"He's a coming here to the apartment?" Thor asked as he rose from the bed and pushed the blanket away.

"I don't think so, but it looks like he knows the general location you're in, and he's started going through the supernatural community there, too. He wants to find Cecil, and he's not going to stop."

Thor already knew that, but he hadn't thought Fabrice would be able to find Cecil. "How close is he?"

"As far as know, he's nowhere close to you, but I wanted to tell you anyway."

"You were right. I needed to know."

"Thor? What happened?" Cecil asked in a sleepy voice.

Thor patted Cecil's thigh before turning his attention back to the phone. "I'll call you back tomorrow morning. Thanks for letting me know."

"Call me if anything happens. I'll freak out enough as it is."

"I will." Thor hung up and turned toward Cecil, who looked more awake than his voice had hinted at. "Fabrice is in Scotland."

Cecil's eyes went round. "In Scotland? How did he find us? Do we have to leave?"

"Not yet. We can talk about it tomorrow morning, but Tryg doesn't think Fabrice knows exactly where we are. We'll be fine for the rest of the night, but we should leave first thing tomorrow morning."

"How?" Cecil asks again.

Thor didn't know how to answer that. He hadn't thought it was possible for someone to find a dream-walker, or to touch them in the dream world. He didn't know how Fabrice was doing it, or even if Cecil was safe there, but he trusted Tryg. If Tryg had told him to leave right now, he would have. As it was, he and Cecil could probably sleep another few hours before packing and running. They would need the sleep, if Fabrice was coming after them.

"I shouldn't have dream-walked," Cecil said, already blaming himself for what was happening.

"You don't know if that's how he found you."

"How else? It's the only way he could have. He managed to strangle me in the dream world. It's not a stretch to think it's how he found me."

Thor sighed and dragged Cecil into his arms. He kissed Cecil's forehead. "It's no use obsessing over this right now. We should try to sleep for another few hours. We can talk in the morning and decide if we should go to another safe place." But if Fabrice could find them there, what was to say he wouldn't find them anywhere they went?

CHAPTER ELEVEN

Cecil hadn't been able to sleep, not after Tryg's phone call. He'd tried, and he was pretty sure Thor had fallen asleep at one point, but he'd spent the rest of the night staring at the ceiling.

Fabrice had found him. He might not know precisely where Cecil was, but he knew where to look, and once again, nothing and no one would stop him. Cecil didn't know any details, not yet, but it wasn't hard to understand what was happening. Just like he'd done in Brussels, Fabrice was torturing and interrogating people in the supernatural community to get to Cecil. He wouldn't stop until he got to him, and Cecil was starting to wonder if he should give himself up. Having hours to think about that while Thor gently snored beside him hadn't helped Cecil make a decision.

He didn't want to give himself up. He knew what would happen to him if he did. He'd been trying to avoid it for decades. What was the alternative, though? He could continue running and hoping Fabrice wouldn't get to him and watch his brother tear apart the paranormal communities in half Europe, or he could make it stop. He could protect the people who had nothing to do with this and make sure Fabrice didn't hurt anyone else. But how was he going to do that? There was no way Thor would allow him out of his sight, not now that Fabrice was almost on them. Thor was going to make sure Cecil was okay, safe and sound, and that meant he'd notice it if Cecil left.

Thor's phone chirped, startling Cecil and waking Thor up.

Thor reached for it, turning it off as he stretched. He turned toward Cecil and asked, "You slept okay?"

Cecil's heart felt like it squeezed in his chest. He didn't know when it had happened, but somewhere along the way, he'd started caring for Thor, and Thor had started caring for him. That was one of the reasons Thor wouldn't allow Cecil to give himself up. He'd taken it upon himself to be Cecil's protector, and he'd take it as a personal offense if anything happened to him.

"Cecil?" Thor asked as he rose to prop himself up on his elbow.

Cecil blinked. His eyes burned, but he forced himself to focus on the moment. "I'm fine. I didn't get much sleep, but I didn't expect to, not after that phone call."

"You stayed awake the rest of tonight?"

"Most of it."

Thor's expression softened. He reached out and gently stroked Cecil's cheek. "You should have woken me up."

"You needed the rest." Especially if Fabrice was going to find them before they left the apartment. They still didn't understand how he'd found out they were in Scotland, so anything was possible.

"So did you." Thor kissed Cecil's forehead. "Come on. We need to get up and start moving. I want to be out of here as soon as possible. I'm hoping we'll be able to get far enough away before Fabrice realizes we're not in the country anymore that he won't be able to find us again."

Thor's easy affection startled Cecil and made him feel flustered. Cecil hadn't expected that from a man he barely knew and who was clearly more used to living on his own than sharing his apartment. "We still don't know how he found us to begin with. What if he finds us again? What if he follows us wherever we go?" What if Fabrice being able to find them was Cecil's fault?

He'd insisted on dream-walking even though he'd known it wouldn't change anything. Talking to Fabrice never had. He was so angry with Cecil and his mother that he wouldn't trust Cecil, not ever. He wouldn't give Cecil a chance. The only thing he wanted when it came to Cecil was for Cecil to die as painfully as possible. That was what Cecil was going to have to face if he gave himself up.

But maybe it was worth it.

Cecil logically knew it wasn't his fault, but he couldn't help feeling guilty knowing that so many people were hurting and dying when he could prevent it, even if it meant his death.

Thor had rolled out of bed while Cecil was thinking, and he'd disappeared into the bathroom. He came out of it, still drying his face, his piercings glinting in the morning light. "Cecil? I don't want to rush you, but we need to get out of here."

Cecil sighed. He knew that. He knew he and Thor needed to leave before Fabrice got there—because he was going to get there. Cecil wasn't sure of much right now, but that, he knew.

He got out of bed and headed toward the bedroom door. Thor stopped him before he could leave, wrapping his fingers around Cecil's arm to stop him. "It's not your fault," he said.

Cecil closed his eyes. He'd hoped Thor wouldn't bring that up. He knew Thor was thinking about it, of course, but he'd managed to avoid talking about it last night, and he wanted things to continue that way. Thor wouldn't give up easily, though. He'd given Cecil time yesterday, but now, he needed Cecil to be objective about the situation.

Cecil didn't think they meant that in the same way, though. Thor wanted him to realize that what Fabrice was doing wasn't his fault, and he did. But he also realized that Fabrice wasn't going to stop until he got what he wanted. Cecil could let that happen, or he could find a way to stop Fabrice.

He swallowed and forced himself smile so Thor wouldn't

realize where his thoughts had been ever since Tryg had called last night. "I know."

"Do you? Because you look like you're about to do something stupid."

Cecil couldn't allow Thor to find out what he was thinking about. "I'm not. I'm sorry if I'm not looking forward to running again and I can't forget about the people Fabrice has been killing to get to me." He knew he was being snappish, but he didn't feel like keeping Thor happy. He didn't feel like happiness was going to be part of his life ever again. It was probably a dire outlook on life, but it felt realistic.

Thor didn't let go. "I know it's difficult to deal with this, but it will be harder if you think it was your fault. You couldn't have done anything to stop your brother."

Yes, he could have. He probably was going to once he got over the fear. He couldn't think about it right now, not when Thor might realize what he was thinking about, but he was going to. The sooner this situation was over, the better it would be for everyone — except Cecil, but he was getting used to that idea.

It was going to hurt. He was aware of that. Fabrice would take his anger for Cecil and their mother out on Cecil. It had been growing for years — decades — and he'd had a lot of it to begin with. But once he was done, Cecil would be free. He'd be dead, and no doubt relieved. Fabrice wouldn't hurt anyone else to get to him. He would probably continue torturing and killing people, but there was nothing Cecil could do about that. He could stop Fabrice from killing people in his search for him, but he'd never had any kind of influence on the rest of his brother's life.

Cecil cleared his throat. "We should go."

Thor frowned. "We're going to, but I need to know you're not going to do something stupid."

"The only person I'm leaving this place with is you. I

promise." Cecil didn't say anything about the next place where they would stay. He didn't even know where that was, so he had no way to plan things. That was okay. Planning would probably mean that Thor would realize what he was doing. It would be better to act on instinct so Thor couldn't get any hint that Cecil was going to leave.

He wished Thor would leave him behind. Any sane person would, but Thor had decided he was going to be Cecil's protector, and from the little Cecil knew about him, once he made a decision, he stuck to it. Cecil had no idea why Thor had latched on to him, but the *why* didn't matter. Cecil was going to make sure Thor was okay by giving himself up to Fabrice and making sure Fabrice didn't hurt him.

Cecil was planning something, the little shit. Thor knew it, even though he didn't know what it was. He was going to find out, though, but not now. Now, he needed to get Cecil out of the apartment before Fabrice somehow found him. Thor couldn't wait to kick the guy's ass, but that wouldn't happen until he was sure Cecil was okay, and he couldn't make sure of that if Fabrice attacked now.

"Ready?" he asked Cecil.

They were standing in the living room next to the door that led to the balcony. Thor had turned the alarm on, and he always left the place through the balcony. It made it harder for people to keep track of him when they didn't notice him coming and going.

"As ready as I can be, I guess."

Cecil sounded sad and worried, and while Thor fully understood why that was, he wished he could do something to change that. Maybe once this mess was over, he could take Cecil somewhere for a vacation. He knew Cecil had traveled a lot since his brother had started trying to kill him, but that no doubt had been anything but a relaxing vacation. Cecil deserved to spend his days doing whatever he wanted without having to look behind his back to make sure his brother hadn't found them. He deserved to relax and not have to think about anything that would stress him out.

That wasn't going to happen until Thor took care of Fabrice, and that meant he would have to do it sooner rather than later. Getting rid of Fabrice might mean that Cecil would leave Thor behind, and while it wasn't something Thor wanted, he was ready to go through that if it meant Cecil would be happy and safe. That was the only thing Thor considered important in this situation. His own feelings didn't matter, not when Cecil's life and happiness were in the balance.

Thor pressed a fingertip under Cecil's chin and tilted his head up so they could look at each other. "You're going to be okay," he promised. He would keep that promise, whatever happened.

"I might, but what about everyone else?"

Thor sighed. He'd known that was where Cecil's thoughts were. That was why Cecil was thinking about doing something stupid. He cared about people he didn't even know, more than he cared about his own well-being. That was going to get him killed, and Thor wouldn't let that happen. He didn't tell Cecil that, though. Instead, he kissed Cecil's forehead and lowered his hands to twine his fingers around Cecil's. "We'll find a way."

"I know," Cecil whispered.

Thor opened his mouth to reassure him more, but something moving in the corner of his vision made him snap his mouth shut. Instead of saying anything, he poofed them into smoke. He could feel Cecil's surprise and shock, but he focused on keeping them together and moving toward the wall. Something crashed into the window in front of which they'd been standing seconds before. Thor hadn't expected it, but he wasn't surprised. Fabrice had found them, and he was there to take Cecil.

Thor wouldn't let him.

He didn't waste time and didn't shift back to his human form, even though he wanted to. He wanted to kick Fabrice's ass, to make sure he understood that he couldn't lay a finger on Cecil without expecting consequences. But Cecil's safety was more important than Thor's need to hurt Fabrice as much as he'd been hurting Cecil, so Thor waited until Fabrice — once again dressed all in black with his face covered — headed toward the hallway that led to the bedrooms before drifting out the window.

How did he find us?

Thor wasn't surprised Cecil had questions. He had them too, but he had no answers to them. He didn't understand how Fabrice had found them. He wasn't sure Cecil was right when he said that Fabrice had probably found them through his dream-walking. He still didn't think that was possible. Of course, the fact that Fabrice had hurt Cecil even though they'd been in the dream world wasn't something Thor had thought possible either. How had Fabrice managed that? He could have found a way to follow Cecil in the dream world to his physical position, but if so, why hadn't he come right to them? He'd spent time asking questions and torturing people to find Cecil, enough time that's Cecil and Thor had been able to finish sleeping through the night and have breakfast before packing. Wouldn't he have come straight to them if he knew where Cecil was?

Thor thought he would have, and that meant he hadn't known. He'd been aware that Cecil was in Scotland, but he hadn't known exactly where.

I don't know, Thor told Cecil. But he would find out. He didn't know how, and it wasn't going to happen soon because he needed to get Cecil to safety, but he'd do it.

Fabrice reappeared in the living room. Thor didn't think he knew that Cecil was traveling with a draugr, and he didn't want him to find out for as long as possible. He and Cecil could easily sneak out in his smoke form, but Fabrice might find a way to counter if he knew that was what they were doing. Thor needed to make sure Fabrice was going to stay in the apartment for a bit. Hopefully, he'd wait and see if Cecil came back, but just in case, Thor decided to give him a push in that direction.

Using the power that he had over the elements, Thor created a storm. It wasn't difficult, not in Scotland. All the elements were already there, and Thor only had to focus them on the area around the apartment building. He gave them strength, enough to create a strong storm that would make it hard for anyone to move. He didn't know how Fabrice had gotten to the apartment, but he doubted it was on foot. Fabrice was going to have a hard time driving through this.

Did you do that? Cecil asked.

Yes. I told you I had powers over the elements.

I know, but I didn't expect it to be like this. It's impressive. It's very . . . like you.

Like me?

Yes. You kind of came into my life like a storm, you know? Strong and impressive and deadly, but also soothing.

Thor might have puffed out his chest if he'd been in his human form, which was ridiculous. *It's useful to distract Fabrice. I don't know how long it's going to work, but it should give us enough time to go.*

It didn't need to work for long, though.

Thor drifted them away from the storm and the building. He knew where they were going. He'd been planning from the first time Fabrice had attacked. He'd suspected Fabrice wasn't going to let this go, so he'd known they wouldn't be able to stay in one place for too long. He owned a lot of apartments all over the world, but since he and Cecil were flying, he couldn't choose one that was too far from their current position. He couldn't afford to get too tired, because he needed to be able to defend Cecil in case Fabrice got to them.

Apartments weren't all he owned, though. Iceland wasn't exactly close, but Thor had trained, and he was able to travel over a lot of miles in his smoke form. Cecil's added weight wouldn't slow him down too much, and they'd probably be at his cottage in the south of Iceland by evening. Once there, they could decide what their next step would be—as long as Cecil didn't decide that now was the right moment for him to put his stupid plan in action.

You should rest, he said through their bond.

I don't know if I can.

I'll keep you safe. I promise.

I know. It's not you. I'm just so tired of Fabrice coming after me and having to run and leave everything behind every few weeks. I've been doing it for so long that I can barely remember what my life was like before.

Thor wanted to give him that. He wanted Cecil to have a normal life, or as normal a life as a mage could have. Life for paranormal creatures wasn't often easy, but Thor wanted to do everything in his power to make sure it happened for Cecil, even if it meant reading the future. He didn't enjoy doing it because it wasn't an exact science and most of the time it was too hard to interpret, but Cecil's life was in the balance now, and it was worth trying to understand what the future was attempting to say.

CHAPTER TWELVE

Cecil had made his decision, and it had been surprisingly easy. He'd had more than enough time to think about things while Thor flew them wherever they were going. Cecil had no idea where that was, and he wasn't going to ask. He didn't want to risk Fabrice finding them again because of him. He still didn't know how Fabrice had found them the first time around, so he needed to be more careful than ever. This was the last evening he'd spend with Thor, so he'd only have to be careful for a few more hours. After that, he'd find his way to the closest big city, and he'd make sure Fabrice found him. He hoped he'd get Fabrice's full attention and that Fabrice would forget that someone had been helping Cecil escape until now. The last thing Cecil wanted was for Fabrice to focus on Thor. He was leaving to keep Thor safe.

We're there.

Cecil blinked—could he even do that when he was smoke? Then he looked down. He'd expected another apartment building in a small town, but that wasn't what he was seeing. Instead of an apartment building, the place where he'd be staying with Thor was a small house. It looked like it would fit perfectly in a fairytale, even with all the windows dark. The walls were made of stones, and there were curtains in the windows. It looked like a place where an old grandmother might live, not a pierced Viking hundreds of years old.

Cecil had no idea where the closest city was, and that might be a problem. He would have to deal with it. Maybe he could start walking and hope he'd find somewhere to go. He only needed to get Fabrice's attention. He didn't care where that happened. As long as Fabrice didn't find this house, things would be okay, at least for Thor. That was all that mattered.

What do you think?

Cecil smiled. *I'm not sure how to answer that.*

Not what you expected?

Not at all. It's yours?

Yep. And I love it, more than I like some of the apartments I own.

For some reason, Cecil didn't have a hard time imagining Thor here. It wasn't what he'd expected, but he could see Thor puttering around in the front yard, or reading a book in front of the fireplace, even though he'd never been inside the house. It looked like it was peaceful, and he understood why Thor found it appealing. He wished he could spend more time there, maybe explore the meadow he could barely see behind the house. He wished he could fall asleep tangled with Thor in front of the fireplace. He wished they could cook together in what was no doubt a tiny kitchen.

All of those were pointless dreams. Cecil should stop thinking about them, because it would hurt more if he didn't.

Thor lowered them and slipped under the front door. Cecil was momentarily unbalanced when they turned back to their human form, and he had to hold himself up against the wall. Thor didn't seem to have the same problem, but of course, he was used to traveling that way. Cecil wished he could have the chance to learn, but that had probably been the last trip he'd make as smoke.

"I'm exhausted," Thor muttered as he flipped the light on.

The place looked exactly like him. There was a lot of dark wood, books, and the carpets that looked soft enough to sleep on them. Everything gave a sense of strength but also protectiveness and comfort. It was the way Cecil felt when he was with Thor, and now, when he was in his house.

"I'm sure you're as tired as me," Thor continued. "There are two bedrooms, and you're welcome to use the guest room, but I was hoping you'd want to share mine."

Cecil knew he should say no. He was planning to sneak out while Thor was sleeping, and he wouldn't be able to do that if Thor was wrapped around him. He'd risk Thor waking up and realizing what he was doing, but he didn't want to spend their last night together on his own. He wanted to take advantage of the last few hours they had together instead of being alone in a cold bed. He couldn't, but he also couldn't tell Thor he wanted the guest room. He knew Thor was going to suspect something was up. That was the last thing Cecil wanted, because then Thor would try to stop him. He'd just managed to gather the courage to do this, and one word from Thor would probably be enough for him to change his mind.

Cecil was afraid. He'd been afraid for the past few decades, but the fear had never reached this level. He had to push through it to do this, and that was going to be hard enough without having to fend Thor off.

He cleared his throat. "Of course."

Thor looked like he wanted to say something, but instead, he turned around. "Come on. Let's get something to eat before we go to bed."

The something to eat was frozen bread and beans, but it was more than enough for Cecil. He just needed something warm that would carry him through the night. Watching Thor as he cooked for him made his heart hurt. Even though only a few days had passed, Cecil had started getting used to the domesticity of this. It was more intimate than sex, in a way. It showed Thor cared much more for Cecil than a fuck buddy. He was taking care of Cecil, and Cecil knew he'd be pissed if he realized what Cecil was planning. He'd be right to be. He'd been trying to keep Cecil safe ever since they'd met, and Cecil was about to throw all that out the window.

Cecil detested thinking about what Thor would do or think when he woke up. Would he try to find Cecil? Cecil suspected he would, and that meant Cecil had to be far enough away that Thor wouldn't be able to find him. Hopefully, Fabrice would drag Cecil to his lair as soon as he had him, wherever that was.

"Ready to go to bed?" Thor asked once the dishes were clean.

The room smelled of bread and love, of family and of a place Cecil wanted to spend the rest of his life in. He had to swallow a few times to manage to get the words out. "I, ah, I think I am going to take the guest room after all."

Thor blinked. "What? Why?"

"We're both tired. We also both know that sleeping isn't what we're going to do if we share a bed."

Thor chuckled. "That's true. I can promise to keep my hands to myself if you want, though."

Cecil leaned against Thor's chest and kissed him. The gesture almost made him cry, but he kept the tears in. "I know you would. I still think we need some time on our own. It will be easier to rest better, and I have to admit I'm a little overwhelmed right now. I don't want you to be angry at me, though."

"I could never be angry at you for needing time and space to yourself. I know everything's been confusing and fast-moving. I get it. You can have all the space you need, for as long as you need it. I won't push, but I want you to know that I'm here if you need anything. I know things have been wild, but I like to think that in the madness, we found each other. I don't expect you to want to talk about this right now, but keep it in mind, please. I'm not going anywhere, not as long as you need me, and not as long as you want to be with me."

Yes, Cecil was going to cry his heart out when he went to bed later. He was going to cry, but that wouldn't change his mind. Now more than ever, he was convinced of what he was doing. He needed to keep Thor safe, and that wouldn't happen if he stayed with him. This was the least he could do for Thor after everything Thor had done for him. Thor might have not been able to save Cecil from Fabrice, but he'd given him something Cecil hadn't had in too long—someone who cared for him, the possibility and hope of a new life and a new relationship, and affection that could have become love if they'd had a chance.

But they didn't.

Cecil was up to something. Thor didn't know what, but he was going to find out.

It hadn't taken him long to realize Cecil was planning something. It wasn't the fact that Cecil didn't want to share Thor's bed. Thor would have accepted that without a problem, but he knew something more was happening here. It was obvious from Cecil's behavior. He'd started acting shifty after they'd eaten, or if Thor was being honest, before then. He'd tried to ignore it, but he couldn't anymore. From what he knew about Cecil, Cecil was feeling sorry about what his brother had done, and he was going to try to find a way to fix it.

That probably meant he was going to give himself up to Fabrice—the sacrificing little shit.

Thor wasn't surprised, but he wished Cecil had talked to him before making that decision. Of course he hadn't, because he knew Thor would say no and make sure he didn't sneak out. Which was exactly what he was about to do.

There was no way he was going to let Fabrice touch Cecil in any way, shape, or form.

Thor turned to smoke and left his bedroom through the window. He didn't know when Cecil was planning to leave, but he'd probably wait until he thought Thor was asleep. Hopefully, that wouldn't be long. Thor might not feel the cold in his smoke form, but that didn't mean he wasn't looking forward to a good night's sleep, especially after last night had been interrupted. He was grateful that Tryg had called, because it meant he'd been able to take Cecil out away before Fabrice could find him, but now he was tired, and having Cecil try to sneak out wasn't helping.

Thor drifted down and stopped at the side of the front door. He hung there, waiting, and while he wasn't sure how long he'd been there when the door creaked open, he didn't think it had been long.

Cecil opened the door only enough to could slip out. He closed the door behind himself and paused. Thor wasn't sure why, but he hoped Cecil was having second thoughts. He wanted to help Cecil, but he could only do that if Cecil let him.

Thor shifted into his cat form. He made sure that Cecil heard him as he crashed through the bushes in his direction. Cecil startled, and he looked like he would run for a moment. Then he looked down, and Thor could have sworn he saw him smile.

Thor sat and meowed loudly.

Cecil looked around frantically. "Shh. You're going to wake everyone."

Thor would have rolled his eyes, but he was pretty sure Cecil would have realized he wasn't a cat if he had. He butted his head against Cecil's leg. He wasn't sure Cecil was going to waste time petting him, but he hoped he would. He didn't think Cecil *wanted* to leave. If anything, Cecil probably wanted to stay, but he felt this was something he had to do. He was a protector, even though he hadn't had occasion to do a lot of protection. He'd been running for too long.

Cecil crouched and rubbed the top of Thor's head. "You're cute, but I have things to do."

Thor ignored Cecil's words and purred. He closed his eyes and enjoyed the petting for a moment. He didn't often have a reason to shift, not into a form that wasn't smoke. This felt good, and he didn't want it to end. He needed to kick Cecil's ass, though.

Thor opened his eyes and meowed even louder than before. Cecil almost fell on his ass when he jerked away. "Come on, baby. Don't do this to me."

It was time to confront him. Thor shifted, crossing his arms over his chest as he looked down at Cecil and stood in front of him. Cecil blinked as if he couldn't quite understand what was happening. Thor arched a brow and waited until Cecil climbed back to his feet.

"How did you know?" Cecil asked.

"How *couldn't* I have known? You're a terrible liar."

"And you're very naked."

Thor wasn't going to smile, no matter how much he wanted to. "It happens when I shift."

"Not when you shift into smoke."

"Only when I shift into one of my animal forms. What are you doing, Cecil?"

Cecil shuffled. "We should go inside. You're going to get frostbite."

Thor wasn't looking forward to losing any part of his anatomy to frostbite, so even though it wasn't that cold, he followed Cecil when Cecil opened the door and walked back into the cottage. Cecil made a beeline for the living room. Thor snatched a blanket from the couch and wrapped it around himself. He didn't care about being naked in front of Cecil, but now wasn't the time to be distracted.

"What were you thinking?" Thor asked. He was angry, but he was trying not to sound too harsh. He understood why Cecil was doing this, and he even respected it, even though he thought it was stupid—and even though it terrified him. He probably wouldn't have tried to stop anyone else doing this. He couldn't let Cecil sacrifice himself, though. He couldn't let Cecil kill himself, and that was exactly what he'd been about to do.

Cecil raked a hand through his hair. "You know what I was thinking. I need to do this."

"You don't need to get yourself killed. That's not going to solve anything."

"It's going to make Fabrice stop killing people."

"For how long? He's not killing people to get to you, not really. He's killing people because he enjoys it. You're only giving him a reason to hide behind, but I doubt he'll stop even if you're gone. You told me yourself that he kills people for their powers. He's not going to stop because he has yours. He'll always want more, and once you're gone, there will be no one ready to stop him."

Cecil wrung his fingers together. "I can't do anything for anyone. He's too strong. I can't even save myself, so how can I save anyone else?"

Thor's heart felt like it was swelling, which was a weird sensation, to say the least. Cecil was too good for this world. Thor didn't understand how he'd survived until now. He reached out, opening his arms, and he was only partly surprised when Cecil came without hesitation. They wrapped around each other, and Thor didn't know what to say. Telling Cecil that his brother wasn't going to stop hurting people even when he was dead probably wasn't helping. Thor needed to make Cecil see he had so many things to live for and that he'd have the occasion to do that once Fabrice had been taken care of. For now, this was nebulous. It was probably hard for Cecil to realize what his life would be like once Fabrice was gone. Thor wanted to give him something to live for, and that meant making himself vulnerable.

He kissed the top of Cecil's head and closed his eyes. "It's been hundreds of years since I cared about someone the way I care about you. I'm selfish. I don't want to lose you, to lose the chance we have at being together. The way I feel about you isn't something I can ignore. I don't want to ignore it. I want to live it, to give us a chance."

"I can't stand by while Fabrice hurts people," Cecil muttered against Thor's chest.

"Then we'll find a way to stop him." He hadn't said no. He hadn't said he wanted to be with Thor, but he also hadn't said no.

"How? I've been looking for a way to stop him for decades."

"But you didn't have me back then. You didn't have Tryg and Isaac. We're on your side this time, and together, we'll find a way." And if they didn't, Thor would.

He wasn't afraid of Fabrice. He understood why Cecil was, but that wasn't going to stop him. He wanted to confront Fabrice, even though he knew nothing he could say would stop him. He wanted to get the feel of the man he'd have to kill sooner rather than later. Cecil wouldn't be happy about that, but Thor felt it was necessary. Fabrice would never stop hunting Cecil, and that meant Thor had to hunt him.

CHAPTER THIRTEEN

Cecil would be pissed if he knew what Thor was about to do.

Thor had put him to bed after they'd had their conversation in the living room. Cecil was exhausted, and it hadn't taken him long to fall asleep. Thor had waited until he was sure Cecil wasn't going to wake up, then he'd rolled out of bed and had gone to the guest room. Now he was lying in the middle of the bed facing the ceiling.

He didn't like dream-walking. He didn't like reading the future. The first one felt like an invasion of privacy, and usually, he didn't want to see what the people he was reaching out to were dreaming off. He never dream-walked into a good person's dreams, not with his job, and when people were nasty in real life, they usually were in their dreams, too. The future-reading, on the other hand, always felt too insecure to be useful. Anything could change the future Thor read, from someone deciding not to kill someone else to someone picking a peanut butter sandwich over a steak.

He was still going to do it. He hoped he wouldn't be forced into reading the future, but he'd do it if it came to that.

He closed his eyes and let his mind drift. He knew Cecil used herbs to help with focus, but he didn't need them. He was so used to doing this that it was like second nature. He might not like it, but it often came in handy, especially when he'd still be working as an assassin.

He knew the exact moment he fell asleep and wasn't in the real world anymore.

Fog surrounded him. It felt welcoming, as if Thor belonged there with it. And maybe he did. He wasn't exactly human anymore. He hadn't been in a long time. Maybe he didn't belong in the human world as much as he belonged here. Not that it mattered. Nothing was going to keep him from Cecil, not even the dream world.

Thor ignored the familiar feeling of Cecil's mind. He recognized it, and it was tempting to drift toward him and see what he was dreaming about. Thor wasn't about to invade Cecil's privacy, though, and he had other things to do. He was there to find Fabrice and to talk to him, and that was what he would do.

Cecil's presence so close to him was helpful, though. Since Fabrice was his brother, it would be easier for Thor to find him than it usually was. Fabrice's mind was probably nothing like Cecil's, but it would have a familiar taste to it. Thor wasn't quite sure how else to explain it. He recognized Fabrice's mind because he recognized the bond he shared with Cecil.

Fabrice was asleep. That probably meant he was close by, enough that it was nighttime for him, too. He did feel a bit like Cecil, but it was only superficial. Once Thor stepped into Fabrice's dream, into his mind, he saw how different the brothers were.

Cecil was soft and gentle, yet strong and brave. The only thing Thor got from Fabrice's mind were negative feelings. There was hatred, yearning for power, the feeling of being better than everyone else, and wanting to be recognized as such. Fabrice really thought he was doing the right thing, at least for himself. He didn't care about anyone but Fabrice, just like Thor had suspected. Killing Cecil and taking his power wouldn't change that. Once he had that power, he'd want another one, then another one.

"Who are you?"

Thor wasn't surprised that Fabrice had noticed him there. He also wasn't surprised they were in what looked like a palace. Cecil had told him about that, and about the signs of decay he was sure were there. They were hidden well, but Thor knew what he was looking for, and he had experience in this—hundreds of years of experience more than Cecil.

Fabrice was behind Thor. This time, he wasn't wearing a mask, and Thor saw him for the first time.

He looked a bit like Cecil. They shared the same red eyes and the same curly brown hair. It would be easy to mix them up in the dark if one didn't know them well. But Thor had spent enough time with Cecil to know him, and there was no way he'd mix the brothers up. Fabrice was harder. He was a cruel man, and that showed in the harsh curl of his lips and in the way he was looking at Thor.

Thor crossed his arms over his chest. "I thought you'd be taller."

Fabrice's eyes widened for a second. "I asked who you are."

"And I told you I thought you'd be taller. I don't know why I always expect evil people to be tall."

Fabrice's eyes narrowed. "You're here for Cecil."

"A gold star for you."

"You're the reason he keeps disappearing on me."

"The reason he keeps disappearing is that he doesn't want to die."

Fabrice stepped closer. "What are you?"

"None of your business. I want you to leave your brother alone."

Fabrice snorted. "That's not going to happen. You should rethink which brother you support. I can give you a lot more than whatever Cecil is giving you."

The thought of falling in love with Fabrice the way he was

falling in love with Cecil was enough to give Thor the heebie-jeebies. "I don't want anything from you."

"Then why are you here? You have to want something. You wouldn't be dream-walking in my mind otherwise."

"I already told you, I want you to leave Cecil alone."

"And I told you that wasn't going to happen. He has something that belongs to me, and I'm going to take it back."

"Your mother would have given you her powers if she'd wanted you to have them."

Fabrice's eyes widened. "He told you about that. Who are you? Who are you to Cecil?"

Thor wasn't about to answer that. "What do you want to leave your brother alone?"

"Nothing you can offer me will ever be enough. Whatever the reason you're here, it's not going to work. I'm not going to stop until I have my mother's powers." He tapped a fingertip on his chin. "What are you? Not a hag. I'd know if you were. I don't know how many creatures can dream-walk, but there are a few."

Thor didn't want Fabrice to find out what he was. He didn't care, but he wanted to keep his powers a secret. It would come in handy if he needed a secret weapon to kill Fabrice.

"But you're not going to tell me, are you?" Fabrice asked.

He stepped closer to Thor, and Thor had to resist the urge to take a step back. He didn't want Fabrice to think he was afraid, because he wasn't.

Fabrice was still close enough to touch Thor, and he did. It's made Thor want to push him away and take a shower, but he stayed where he was and ignored the fingertips that were climbing up his arm.

"What are you to Cecil?" Fabrice asked. He already knew the answer. That much was obvious.

Thor limited himself to arch a brow.

Fabrice smiled. "So that's what Cecil gives you. I'm surprised he knows how it works. From what I know, he hasn't seen any action in bed in a while. I'm sure I'd be better at it than him, and I come with other perks. I could give you a sample right now, and I promise you'll get more once you hand me my brother."

This was going nowhere. It was obvious Thor could have avoided coming here. He'd needed to be sure, though, and now, he was. Nothing he could do or say would change Fabrice's mind, just like he'd expected.

He stepped away, and Fabrice's hand fell to his side. Thor didn't say anything else. He turned around and walked away into the fog. He heard Fabrice call him, but he ignored him. They had nothing else to say to each other.

CHAPTER FOURTEEN

Cecil wasn't surprised to wake up alone in bed. He'd expected Thor to be angry with him after what he'd done. Was he? He would be if their roles were reversed. He'd been afraid that Thor would change his mind — and he had, so he'd been right.

He didn't know where Thor was. The bedroom was empty, but he could smell the scents of breakfast and coffee coming from the open door. Thor had woken up early, and he'd started on breakfast.

Cecil wasn't sure how to deal with things this morning. He was going to apologize, that was for sure, but what else? Would Thor be angry at him? How was Cecil going to deal with that? He also needed to apologize for almost a dream-walking into Thor's mind last night.

He hadn't done it, but it had been a close thing. He'd felt Thor's mind so close to his, almost calling out to him. He'd wanted to dream-walk there, to make sure Thor wasn't pissed at him, to see what Thor was dreaming about. It would have been an invasion of privacy, and he'd stayed away, but he couldn't deny he'd wanted to.

Cecil groaned and rolled to his back. He had so many things to apologize for. He should get a move on so he could get them out of the way. Once that was done, they needed to start talking about finding a way to get rid of Fabrice. He knew they needed to kill him. He didn't like the thought, but it was their only option. He didn't know how they would do it, but that was why he and Thor needed to talk.

And that was why he needed to get up and go downstairs. The sooner he apologized, the sooner they could start planning.

The scene that greeted Cecil in the kitchen was one he knew by now. Thor was cooking, his back to Cecil. He didn't turn around when Cecil walked in, but he pushed a full cup of coffee along the counter. Cecil nodded his thanks and took it. It was the way he liked it, and he hoped it was a sign that Thor was at least ready to talk.

Cecil sat at the table and sipped on his coffee. He waited until Thor was sitting in front of him, already eating his eggs and bacon, to say, "I'm sorry."

Thor blinked. "What are you sorry for?"

"For trying to do this on my own. For not talking to you about it. For almost walking into your dreams last night. I'm sorry about that, by the way. I didn't do it, but it was tempting, even though I know that's private. I shouldn't have done it."

Thor put his fork down. He looked amused, and Cecil wasn't sure he understood why. "You almost walked into my dreams?"

"Almost, yes. I know it's none of my business, so I didn't, but—"

"You don't have to apologize for something you didn't do. Besides, I wouldn't have minded if you'd walked into my dreams."

"You wouldn't have?"

"I have nothing to hide. You already know what I do for a living, and you've lived with me long enough to know I'm a messy kind of guy. You know I killed a lot of people, that I'm very old, and that I'm not human. What else could I want to hide?"

When he put it like that, Cecil understood better. "I'm still sorry."

"Then be sorry for almost getting yourself killed for nothing. I dream-walked into your brother's mind last night."

Cecil almost dropped his mug. "You did *what?*"

"I dream-walked into your brother's mind. I wanted to see him."

"Why would you want to see him? You already know what he's doing."

"I was curious. I thought that maybe by talking to him, I would be able to find a way to make him stop. I know you don't like the thought of killing him, and I don't want you to get hurt, physically or emotionally. I wanted to find another way."

"But killing him is the only way to solve this."

Thor nodded. "You're right. It is. I asked him what he wanted in exchange for leaving you alone, and he didn't have an answer. He wants you to suffer for what your mother did, even though you had no say in it, and he's not going to stop until he gets his revenge. That's a fact, and nothing we can do or say will change it. You have to get used to it."

Cecil was starting to. He'd been running from his brother long enough to know that everything Thor had said was true. He'd been ready to sacrifice himself to save other people's lives, but he wasn't going to do it for nothing. "What's next, then?"

"I'm going to try reading the future."

Cecil hadn't expected that. He knew how little Thor enjoyed doing that, and how useless that ability could be most of the time. "You have no way to be sure that the future you'll see is the one you need to see." Cecil might not have that ability, but that didn't mean he hadn't studied it. He was aware of how unreliable it was, and of the reservations they needed to put into this if they decided to do it.

"I know how this works, Cecil. This isn't going to be the first time I do it."

"I know that. I'm just trying to say that I'm not sure we should do it. I know you don't like it, and if it's not going to be useful . . ."

"We don't know if it's going to be. We don't know anything right now. This is just another weapon we have that we can use against your brother. I'm not going to discard it just because I don't like doing it, not when it might be useful. I'm ready to try every avenue to have you still standing when this is over."

Cecil wasn't sure why he was so against this. It wasn't like Thor risked being hurt while doing it. He wouldn't move from the bed, or the couch, or wherever he decided to do this. He wasn't going into anyone else's mind. He'd be safe in the cottage, with Cecil to watch over him. There was no reason not to do this, and every reason to do it.

Cecil sighed. "All right. What's do you need me to do?"

"I just need you to keep an eye on me. Nothing can happen to me while I'm reading the future, at least not in my mind. It would be easy for someone to get the drop on me, though. I want to be able to defend myself while I'm reading, and that's what I need you to do."

Cecil looked down at himself. "I'm not sure I'll be useful when it comes to defending anything."

"You can wake me up if anything happens, but I don't expect anything to go wrong. No one knows we're here, not even Tryg. There's no way for your brother to find out, at least not in such a short length of time. We'll be safe for a bit in the cottage, so you can relax."

Cecil couldn't remember the last time he allowed himself to relax. He doubted he'd be able to until Fabrice had been dealt with. He still nodded. He didn't need Thor to worry about him, not when he was going to have something else to worry about shortly. What's it like? When you read the future?" No matter how much Cecil had studied the ability, he still had no way to know what it felt like.

"It's almost like watching a movie. There's an image in my mind, and I can try moving backward or forward or even change to another movie. But it's like you're doing it on a crappy TV. It rarely lets you do exactly what you need to do, and when it does, everything is still very confusing. You need to interpret everything you see as if you're seeing it in another language. Some things are clear, and some, usually the ones you need, aren't. Then, of course, there is the fact that the future shifts continuously. Every decision we make, everything we do, changes it. That's why it's so unreliable."

"You make it sound like we're not going to get anything useful out of this."

"We probably aren't, but that won't stop me from trying. I'm going to do everything in my power for you make it out of this alive, Cecil. I already told you that."

And Cecil believed him.

Thor despised reading the future.

It wasn't just that he had to focus in a way he wasn't used to. He also despised the results. Not only could his power show him a future that might not happen, but it also always left him with a headache. Not that it mattered. He was going to do this, and he was more than willing to deal with a headache if it meant reassuring Cecil. He wasn't about to risk having Cecil leave him again and throw himself into danger. Once was more than enough. Thor wasn't sure his heart could take a second time.

"Do you have everything you need?" Cecil asked.

Thor had settled in the guest room. Cecil wasn't using it anyway, and Thor didn't want to do this in the bedroom. He had no idea what he would see, and he didn't want to associate his bed — his space — with bad memories. Hopefully, the future he was going to see would be a good one, even though he had no means of knowing whether it would happen. He wasn't sure how he'd react if the future he was about to see was a bad one for Cecil.

He didn't care much if something happened to him. Thor had lived a long time, and he'd gotten used to the thought of dying one day. It might be nearly impossible for him to be killed, but that didn't mean it wouldn't happen, eventually. Heroes were scouring the earth looking for people like Thor, and someday or other, they would catch up with him. He'd made his peace with that.

What he hadn't made his peace with was the thought of Cecil dying.

He looked at Cecil, so fragile looking yet so strong. Cecil wouldn't have a problem going on without Thor. He'd been alone for most of his recent life. He hadn't needed Thor until now, and he wouldn't need him after this was over. Thor forced himself to smile in an attempt to reassure Cecil. "I have everything I need."

Cecil wrinkled his nose. "You know, it's not fair that you can do this without any help while I have to rely on candles, gemstones, and whatnot."

"It's a question of practice. Even though I don't do this often, I've had hundreds of years to learn the power. I've been doing this for longer than you've been alive, and you've been alive for a while."

Cecil's lips quirked. "Are you calling me old?"

Thor barked out a laugh. "If you're old, then I'm positively ancient." Thor knew he was, and most days, he felt like it. Now wasn't the time to bring this up, though. He cleared his throat. "Now, I'm going to start. From your point of view, it will look as if I'm in a trance, maybe meditating. That's perfectly normal, and I don't want you to worry if it takes me a while to wake up. I have no idea what I'm going to see or how long it's going to take for me to see it. And once I see it, I'm going to try poking at it and looking at it from different angles to be sure I'm getting everything I need to see."

Cecil's smile widened, even though he still looked worried. "That's a lot of seeing."

Thor rolled his eyes. "It's not like I have anything else to do. The point of reading the future is to see it, after all." But he liked that Cecil was teasing him. It made him feel like they were close, probably closer than they really were, and he wasn't thinking about the sex.

In the first time since forever — or that was what it felt like anyway — Thor wanted more. He wanted more time with Cecil. He wanted more than they already had. That would only happen if he made sure that Fabrice never hurt Cecil, so he needed to stop wasting time.

He wiggled a bit until he found a more comfortable position. He never liked sitting cross-legged, but this was the easiest way for him to meditate and to enter the state of mind necessary for him to read the future. Even after all these years, he didn't understand how this power worked. Was he going into another dimension, another plane, like when he dreamwalked? Or did he stay in his mind? He knew his body stayed right where it was, but not where his mind went. Not that it mattered. He didn't care how it worked, as long as it did.

He closed his eyes and regulated his breathing. He tried to think of nothing as he accessed his power. It wasn't easy. It never had been. But for Cecil, he could do it.

It was like a movie Thor could see on the back of his eyelids. He saw Cecil, smiling and laughing. He saw him holding hands with someone, cuddling the man and being obviously happy with him. It was the future, since Thor couldn't see the past, but there was no way for him to tell when that future would happen — if it happened at all. He couldn't see the other man's face, and even his body was slightly blurry. That meant Thor couldn't identify him, and he wasn't sure how he felt about that. He couldn't even tell if it was him, no matter how hard he tried. As far as he knew, this could be the future in half an hour or maybe an hour. He needed to see a more distant future, a future that possibly happened after Fabrice's death. He had no way to guide himself, though, so he kept on watching.

He looked around, trying to find something that could help him identify the moment in which this would happen. Cecil and his man were on the couch, possibly watching TV, since they were both staring at the same spot. There were books on the coffee table, and Thor's heart stuttered when he thought he recognized the cottage. That meant Cecil had to be with him, right? Although since he was planning to leave the cottage to Cecil if anything happened to him, maybe not. But along with the books and the two phones and coffee table, Thor noticed a newspaper.

He moved closer. The newspaper was folded, and he'd never learned to read the local language, but he could read the date. It was a newspaper that would be published six months from now.

Thor relaxed. He still had had no way to be certain that Cecil was with him, although he liked to think so. There was also no way for him to know what had happened to Fabrice. It didn't look like he was still hunting Cecil, considering how different the cottage was, how it looked lived in and not like a hiding place, but like always, there were no certainties when Thor read the future.

He chose to believe that this was a future in which Cecil would have the possibility to be happy. That meant that any moment from now to six months in the future, Fabrice would be dealt with. Thor didn't know who would do it or how it would happen, and he didn't care. He wasn't going to wait around hoping someone else did this for him.

He'd been angry at Cecil for sneaking out and attempting to do things on his own, but he was about to do the same thing. He needed to make sure that this future happened for Cecil, whether or not the other man was him. He needed to be proactive about this and stop running. Fabrice didn't know he was a draugr, so Thor had the element of surprise on his side. He needed to take advantage of that, and that meant leaving Cecil behind so he wouldn't get hurt.

Even if the man wasn't Thor, Thor was happy to see that Cecil had a future. He wanted Cecil to be happy, and he was ready to sacrifice himself for that to happen. Besides, it wasn't like Fabrice could kill him. Fabrice wasn't a hero, and heroes were the only ones who could do that. Even if Thor knew that going alone was probably stupid, he'd be fine. He might get hurt, but it would be worth it if he and Cecil could stop running—if they could have the future that was still happening in front of him.

Chapter Fifteen

Cecil had spent too long staring at Thor. He'd expected this to be quick, but it was anything but. After a few hours, he'd left Thor in the guest room to get lunch ready. He'd eaten, had watched a bit of TV, had read, and Thor was still reading the future. Since Cecil didn't know how long Thor would be like that, he'd decided to get dinner ready.

Was the length of the reading a sign of anything? Cecil should have asked that question before, but he hadn't thought about it. Thor hadn't been able to tell him a lot about how his power worked. It wasn't that Cecil hadn't been curious, but rather, that Thor hadn't known. Cecil didn't mind. He'd have a hard time explaining how he did some of the things he did. Even explaining to Thor, Tryg, and Isaac how he could manipulate death hadn't been easy. He'd tried because Tryg had needed him to, but he would have gladly avoided it. Some things didn't make sense when you're tried to explain them.

But how long it was taking for Thor to do this was making Cecil nervous. He didn't know if the length was a good or bad thing. He knew Thor wanted to analyze everything he saw to be sure he got everything he needed, but still, he'd been under for a long time.

Cecil wasn't even sure if he wanted to find out what Thor had seen. He thought he wanted to ask for it, but that was probably more curiosity than wanting to know what his future would be like. He was terrified at the thought that he might not have a future. If he didn't, then he also didn't want to find out. He didn't want to know if Fabrice was going to die. He knew it was a possibility and a strong one at that. It was like one of those silly prophecies — one of them had to die for the other to survive, or something like that. Of course, in their case, Fabrice would be okay even if Cecil didn't die. The other way around was spot on, though.

Cecil had accepted the fact that his brother would have to die for him to make it. He hated the thought, but he wasn't going to bury his head in the sand. That would only get him killed. Fabrice wanted him dead, and he wouldn't stop for anything to obtain that. The only way for Cecil to make it out alive would be to kill his brother. Thor had been right all along, even though Cecil had refused to see it.

He just hoped that the future Thor was still watching would agree with that.

He left the stew he'd been heating on the stove and went upstairs to the guest room to check on Thor. Thor was still out of it when Cecil got there, but to Cecil's surprise, when he reached out to cup Thor's cheek with his hand, Thor's hand raised to cup his.

"You're awake," he said, sitting on the edge of the mattress. He wasn't sure *awake* was the right word, but it fit.

Thor swallowed. "I have been for a few minutes. I was trying to come back to reality before I got up to look for you."

"You don't have to explain yourself. I came in to check on you a few times, and I was surprised, that's all." Cecil licked his lips. He wanted to ask what Thor had seen, yet at the same time, he didn't. It felt like he and Thor were in a bubble, protected and shielded, and if he asked, the bubble would burst. He didn't want it to. He wanted to have one last normal evening, one last normal night before his world twisted and he had to face it.

He knew Thor would have none of that, though. That was why he wasn't surprised when Thor said, "I saw you with a man."

Cecil blinked. "A man? Fabrice?"

"No. You were here, with the man. I couldn't identify him, no matter how hard I tried, but you were happy with him, maybe in love. The two of you looked like you were home here."

Cecil dropped his hand to squeeze Thor's. "That means the man was you, right?"

Thor shrugged. "I don't know."

"Who else would I be here with?"

Thor shook his head, and instead of answering the question, he said, "It was six months from now."

Cecil's stomach churned. "That means I'll make it. That Fabrice won't get to me."

"I think so."

"What else did you see?"

Thor shook his head. "That's pretty much it."

"But you were out for most of the day."

"Yeah? That probably explains why I feel like I could eat a horse."

"I cooked dinner. But yes, it's evening. That's all you saw?"

Thor let go of Cecil's hand and stretched his arms over his head. "It is. The sense of time passing while I'm doing this isn't normal. I'm not surprised I was out this long, because I tried to get everything I could from what I saw."

"That's how you realized I was here, at the cottage."

"It is. You said you cooked dinner?"

Cecil was relieved at the change in topic. He believed Thor when he said he hadn't seen anything else and insisting wouldn't change that. Cecil would have to accept that reading the future wouldn't be of any real help in this situation. He hadn't expected it to, but he couldn't deny, at least to himself, he was slightly disappointed. He probably wouldn't feel this way if Thor had told him that the man he'd be with in six months was him. Cecil couldn't imagine being with someone else in only six months, especially in a home that belonged to Thor. But the fact that the man hadn't been identifiable made him nervous.

He tried to ignore that feeling as they settled at the kitchen table. Thor looked like he could use a good night's sleep, and Cecil made sure he was comfortable and that he didn't have to raise a finger. It wasn't a hardship, not when Thor was usually the one taking care of Cecil. It was only right for their roles to be reversed every so often, and Cecil knew how hard this had been on Thor. It might not be the same thing, but he always felt exhausted after he manipulated death. It took a lot of focus, just like reading the future had taken a lot of focus for Thor.

Things seemed to shift as they headed upstairs to bed. They'd shared Thor's bed last night, and Cecil knew Thor expected them to do the same tonight. It would be different, though. Last night, Cecil had snuck out, and Thor had clung to him in his sleep after busting him as if afraid Cecil would attempt to run again. It hadn't been the right time for sex, but tonight was different. And they both knew it. They both could *feel* it.

Cecil felt jittery as he got ready for bed. Their previous encounter in the gym at the apartment had been a spur of the moment thing. Cecil didn't regret it, just like he didn't regret whatever would happen tonight, but this felt different. It felt more thought out, inevitable yet almost like routine — like it was a thing they did every night. Thor was already in bed when Cecil left the bathroom, the light in the bedroom off. The sky was dark outside the window, and Cecil almost fell on his face when he stumbled on a shoe.

"Are you trying to kill me?" he grumbled.

"I wouldn't be able to make love to you if I were." Thor sounded so matter-of-fact, so sure that was what they were about to do, that Cecil was tempted to ask him what he was talking about.

He wanted Thor to make love to him as much as Thor wanted it, though, so he stayed silent, just in case he ruined everything by trying to banter.

"You're not going to make this awkward, are you?" Thor asked. He grabbed Cecil's arms and rolled them so he loomed over Cecil.

Cecil squeaked and instantly regretted it because it had sounded like he was a giant mouse. "What?" he asked, his voice unsteady.

Thor loomed over him, but he didn't make Cecil feel small or vulnerable. "There's no reason to feel awkward. We did this before."

"It wasn't the same."

"Because it wasn't in a bed? That doesn't change anything. I want you as much as I wanted you before, and I won't leave once it's over. I'm here until you don't want me to be anymore."

Or until Fabrice found them, possibly, but neither of them said that, and Cecil didn't want to think about it, especially not once Thor leaned down to kiss him.

It felt both like a last time and a first time. Cecil didn't understand how that was possible, but it did, and he had to force himself to focus on Thor so he wouldn't start thinking this could *be* their last time. It wasn't hard after a while because Thor seemed to know exactly what he needed to do to drive Cecil crazy.

He took his time undressing Cecil. No matter how much Cecil begged him to do something, Thor ignored him and focused on kissing what felt like every single inch of his body until Cecil's legs trembled and he knew they wouldn't hold him up if he tried to stand.

Then Thor got serious, and Cecil thought he might die.

They hadn't talked about who would be in what role, but

Cecil hoped he'd been obvious about the fact that he wanted to be fucked. He preferred it, although he wasn't averse to fucking a man—especially not Thor—whose ass looked like it was made for it. But with the feeling that it might be the last time they did this, Cecil needed to feel Thor inside of him.

"You're so beautiful," Thor murmured as he once again kissed down Cecil's chest, stopping to tease a nipple with his teeth.

"And you're exasperating," Cecil said, his voice rising when Thor's chin bumped against the head of his cock. "Do you have lube? Please tell me you have lube?" He was ready to go downstairs and grab the butter from the fridge otherwise.

"Of course I do." Thor reached between the pillows, and Cecil wondered how he'd managed not to notice the bottle there.

"Good. Now make good use of it. And you better be fast."

Thor pouted, which was an expression Cecil hadn't yet seen on him. It was oddly endearing, and entirely out of place on Thor. He looked glorious, kneeling there between Cecil's open legs. Cecil had known about the piercings, of course, but during their frantic encounter in the gym, Cecil hadn't realized Thor's cock was pierced, too. A ring glinted on the head, making Cecil feel all wobbly inside. He'd never had a lover with a pierced cock, and he was both wary and eager to find out how that was going to feel inside him.

"It won't hurt you."

Cecil blinked. "What?" God, he sounded like an idiot.

"The piercing. It won't hurt you, and it won't get lost inside of you."

Cecil grunted. "Good. I hadn't thought about that possibility. Now I'm going to worry about it the entire time."

Thor smile was wicked. "No, you're not. You're not going to be able to worry about anything in about five minutes."

He was right—as soon as he put his hands on Cecil, Cecil stopped thinking. Thor felt like he was everywhere at the same time—kissing down Cecil's neck, stroking his cock, fitting fingers inside his ass. Cecil was surrounded, and he *loved* it.

He felt so full when Thor finally entered him that he had to screw his eyes shut for a few seconds and focus on breathing. He was straddling the fine line between pain and pleasure, and he was relieved to find out that Thor was as careful and considerate during sex as he was in the rest of his life. He gave Cecil the time he needed, holding still yet very much present, until Cecil opened his eyes and nodded at him.

It was still painful, but it was nothing Cecil couldn't solider through until pleasure arrived. Having Thor inside him felt like a miracle, something precious he needed to cherish, and he did. He wrapped himself around Thor, both legs and arms anchoring them together as Thor moved.

Cecil wanted to do this for the rest of his life. He didn't care what he'd have to do to make it happen—he'd just make sure it would.

CHAPTER SIXTEEN

Thor wanted to see how Cecil looked when he came, and he wasn't disappointed. Cecil cried out as Thor pushed into him harder and faster, his nails probably leaving scratches in Thor's shoulders. Thor would wear those marks proudly — as soon as he came, anyway. His cock felt like it was about to explode, so he wiggled his hand between him and Cecil to jack Cecil off.

Thor blinked when he suddenly found himself on his back, Cecil perched on top of him. His cock had slid out as they rolled, but Cecil didn't hesitate, grabbing it and keeping it upright as he lowered himself onto it again.

He wanted to be in control, and Thor was more than thrilled to let him take the lead. Besides, it was easier for him to jack Cecil off in this position.

Cecil looked like an apparition. His face and his chest were flushed, and his hair stuck to his forehead, but he kept moving, chasing the pleasure Thor could give him. He bounced on Thor's cock, utterly unashamed.

Thor grinned, and on the next slide down, he pushed up. He knew Cecil would love the feeling of his piercings on his prostate, and while it took him a few thrusts to find it, Thor knew the moment he did. Cecil's back went rigid, and he threw his head back, whimpering. Thor pushed up again, pleasure coiling in his groin, urgent and unstoppable. He ground his hips against Cecil's ass on the next thrust, and Cecil's cock spurted. His ass tightened around Thor, and that was enough for Thor to come.

He screwed his eyes shut when he saw stars and moved his hands to Cecil's hips, holding him in place as he filled him. Knowing that his cum—that a part of him—would be in Cecil for the rest of the night made Thor feel smug and like the knowledge would make it easier for him to sneak out.

He wasn't worried about Cecil waking up, not after that, but he knew that he'd find a dozen reasons why he shouldn't go if he let himself think about it too much.

He couldn't allow himself to do that. He needed to find Fabrice, and he needed to find him now.

Thor waited until Cecil was asleep, still damp from their shower and pink from their lovemaking. He looked like he belonged in Thor's bed, and Thor hoped he'd still be there when he came home. He prayed that he *would* come home and wouldn't allow himself to think otherwise as he left the bedroom, dressed and ready to find Fabrice.

Thor didn't know where to find him, but it wasn't hard for him to dream-walk and locate him. He was only partly surprised to realize that Fabrice was already in the country. Cecil hadn't dream-walked since they'd left Scotland, so it shouldn't have been possible. Thor doubted Fabrice would tell him how he managed to follow them, so he wasn't going to bother asking.

The place where Fabrice was staying looked a bit like the palace where Thor had dream-walked in the attempt to convince him to leave Cecil alone. It was a smaller, less crumbly, but it was too big for one person. Thor was happy about that. The space meant that the neighbors wouldn't hear anything coming from the house. He knew Fabrice wouldn't come easily—or quietly.

Thor shifted back into his human form once he was inside the villa. He didn't know where exactly Fabrice was, but since he was looking for him, he didn't bother trying to hide. He wandered the hallways, not surprised when he found Fabrice sitting in a luxurious office. He doubted Fabrice had any use for the room, but he couldn't deny the man looked good sitting behind the desk in a red velvet and golden wood chair.

"I was just starting to think you weren't going to come," Fabrice said. He tried to look around Thor. "Where is my brother?"

"Somewhere you won't be able to find him."

Fabrice laughed, and the sound was anything but happy. "Hiding him isn't going to save him."

"Maybe not, but I don't think you expected me to bring them here with me."

Fabrice leaned back in his chair. "You're right. I didn't expect you to. I *do* expect him to come running as soon as he realizes I have you, though."

"You talk as if it's a done deal."

"You threw yourself into the lion's den. What do you expect me to do? Allow you to walk out of here freely? Allow you to kill me? Because that's why you're here, isn't it? To kill me. To save my brother from me."

"I wouldn't have to kill you if you'd just leave Cecil alone."

"But that's not going to happen. We both know it."

Of course, Thor knew it. He hadn't come here in the hope of changing Fabrice's mind. He'd come to kill him, and that was what he was about to do.

"I won't lie down and take whatever you're planning to do," Fabrice warned.

"I don't expect you to do that, either, but you have no idea what you put yourself against."

Fabrice chuckled. "Of course I know. I'm not an idiot. You're a draugr."

Thor hadn't expected Fabrice to have realized that, but even though he had, it didn't change anything. "Since you know I'm a draugr, you know there is nothing you can do against me. You can't kill me. You can hurt me, but I'll come again and again until you're dead."

"Oh, I know I can't kill you." He rose from the chair and walked around the desk. "That's doesn't mean I'm not going to try. I've always thought draugr immortality was over-rated."

"It's not."

Thor was ready when Fabrice lunged for him. He grabbed the man's throat and threw him to the side. He hit the shelves there, and books rained over him. He didn't seem to notice, but Thor didn't miss the grimace on his face and the twinge of his back.

Fabrice attacked again. This time, he got a hit in, and Thor felt blood trickle from his lower lip. He didn't pause to check the wound. It was nothing more than a bug bite. He back-handed Fabrice, wondering if the man was hiding some-thing — training, a power he would use against Thor. Nothing happened, though, and every time Fabrice attacked, Thor knocked him down, until Fabrice didn't try to get up again.

Thor stood above him, looking down. "You should give up. I might let you live if you promise you won't touch a hair on Cecil's head again."

Fabrice laughed. His teeth were red with blood, and he spat a blob of bloody saliva on the carpet. "I'm never going to leave him alone. I will take what belongs to me, and then I will kill him. And I will force you to watch as a punishment for what you did today."

Thor snorted. "And how do you think you're going to do that? You've barely managed to make me bleed. You can't kill me, so your fireballs aren't going to be useful. Face it, Fabrice. You can't do anything against me."

Fabrice sat up, his lips twisting. "I might not be able to hurt you, but he can. And he'll do it as soon as I'm done with my brother and not one second before because I want you to watch as I torture Cecil until he begs me to stop."

He looked to the side, and Thor followed his gaze. He sucked in a breath when he saw the man standing in the door frame.

Thor had never seen him, but he didn't need to have to know what the man was. All heroes looked pretty much the same — tall, blond, blue-eyed, and sporting the tattoo of their fraternity on their neck, the black symbol stark against their pale skin. This man wasn't any different, and Thor now knew why Fabrice had been gloating.

He might not be able to kill Thor, but this man could.

Cecil didn't know what had woken him up, but he knew something was wrong.

Then he realized he was still sleeping.

He didn't often dream-walk by accident. Most of the time, it took him focus and having a clear objective in mind to do it. It wasn't unheard for it to happen, though, so apart from the niggle of worry in the back of his mind, he didn't really worry, not right away. Instead, he reached out for Thor's mind. He expected to find it close to him since they were sharing a bed, but he wasn't there.

It could mean anything. Maybe Thor had already woken up and was downstairs cooking breakfast. Maybe he was in the bathroom. But the niggle wouldn't leave, and Cecil had learned a long time ago to trust his instincts.

He tried to ignore the panic bubbling in his chest and focused on Thor.

Thor wasn't asleep. That much, Cecil was sure of. That meant he couldn't dream-walk in Thor's mind, but it didn't mean he couldn't find him. Now that he was close to Thor, he knew what Thor's mind felt like and what he needed to look for in order to get to him. It was hard, though. It shouldn't have been, and it *wouldn't* have been if Thor had still been in the cottage, but Cecil knew he wasn't as soon as he tried to reach out.

Thor had snuck out, damn him.

After kicking Cecil's ass for trying to do things on his own, he'd done exactly that. Cecil was going to kill him as soon as he got his hands on him.

Cecil had no way to know where Thor was in the real world, even after he found him. The dream world was all fog, nothing else. There were no roads, no buildings. Only minds.

Thor's mind felt like a jungle. It felt ancient but welcoming, and while Cecil wanted to take his time exploring, he didn't. It wasn't his place, not when Thor didn't even know he was there. Besides, he had more urgent things to take care of, like trying to understand where Thor was and freeing him. *Because Thor was in trouble.* Cecil had known that since he'd reached out for him and hadn't found him where he was supposed to be. That was what had woken him up. He'd felt something was wrong even though he'd been asleep, and his power had reached out to find Thor.

Cecil had been working on this power of his for a long time. He'd perfected the way of sneaking into people's minds without having them notice it, to get information out of people's minds even when they were awake. It had been necessary for him—for his survival. Now that ability came in handy, because Cecil was able to sneak into the part of Thor's mind where his consciousness was and take a peek.

It was weird.

Cecil hadn't done this often. It felt too intimate, too much as if he were doing something taboo. He probably was. No one in their right mind would allow him to do something like this if they were aware that he could. Thor would probably be angry at him when he told him about it. Not that Cecil cared. The only thing he wanted was to find Thor, and he'd do everything he could to make that happen.

He didn't have to wonder to know what Thor had been thinking when he'd left the cottage. He'd been planning to solve this, and he'd decided to go to Fabrice on his own. In theory, Cecil supposed it could have worked. There was nothing Fabrice could do about Thor's immortality. He couldn't kill Thor, and Cecil didn't doubt that Thor had counted on that. The problem was that Thor didn't know Fabrice as well as Cecil did. Fabrice was sneaky, and he had a way to find out things. He was intelligent and observant.

And from what Cecil could see through Thor's eyes, Fabrice had guessed that Thor was a draugr. There was no other explanation for the man who was holding Thor's arm behind his back.

Cecil sucked in a breath. His brother had caught Thor, and Cecil knew exactly what Fabrice would do.

Then the man behind Thor moved, and Cecil turned his attention to him.

The man moved to the side, and Cecil could tell Thor was being restrained. There was no panic in Thor's mind, though, only regret and worry. Cecil couldn't understand why Thor wasn't afraid. Even Cecil recognized the tattoo on the blond man's neck. He was a hero, the only being who could kill Thor. Cecil was grateful that killing a draugr was complicated and lengthy. It gave him more time, even though he had no clue what he could do with it, not yet.

"I need to take him away," the hero said.

"That wasn't the plan," Fabrice snapped. He never took it well when someone ruined his plans or contradicted him.

"I told you from the beginning that I wasn't going to kill him, not here, not now. He's going to be judged by the hero conclave."

Fabrice snorted. "Judged? He's a draugr. Isn't your job to get rid of him and people like him?"

"It is. But we don't take that job lightly. No matter what he is, he still has a human side, and we need to honor that."

"He's mine, and you know it."

"You're not going to be allowed to keep him and do whatever you have planned with him."

Fabrice stomped his foot. "And who is going to stop me?" He eyed the hero up and down and leered at him. "You're welcome to try, of course." The hero's shoulders tensed, but before he could protest or say anything else, Fabrice said, "How about you stay for the rest of today and tonight? I'm sure you need to rest, and I'm offering you a place to do so. I have room where you can put him in while you eat and sleep. I won't touch him, although I can't promise I won't try to convince you to leave him to me again. He and I have things to settle, and I felt like I did a lot of work for nothing only to have him taken away from me."

Cecil hoped the guy wouldn't believe Fabrice. It was so obvious that he was lying, but Cecil wasn't sure if the hero was aware of it. Fabrice needed the hero and Thor to stay with him.

Cecil was worried. He might be able to take on Fabrice. But an entire conclave of heroes was different — or even only one of them. They were the thing of nightmares for people like Thor and Cecil, and Cecil had no clue if they could be defeated. He knew on his own, he wouldn't be able to do anything, but once he knew where Thor was and that he would stay there for a bit, he could try to do something.

The hero looked like he wanted to say no, but instead, he nodded curtly. "I appreciate this, thank you. I'll make sure the draugr is secure in whatever room you'll allow me to keep him in."

Cecil stayed in Thor's mind for as long as he dared to. He needed to find out where Thor was, but he couldn't ask him. That meant he had to look through Thor's eyes and find a way to understand.

He recognized the house when Thor, the hero, and Fabrice stepped into the entrance. Fabrice and Cecil don't share the same father, and while Cecil's had been a humble man who worked wood, Fabrice's had been a French nobleman. He'd left Fabrice a lot of money, as well as several houses and palaces. Fabrice was in one of them right now, in Great Britain. Cecil had been there once, and he never wanted to go again.

It looked like he'd have to, though.

Now that he knew where Thor was, he needed to leave Thor's mind and start planning. He was wary of doing that, though. He didn't want to leave Thor alone, even though he knew Thor could take care of himself. Of course, the fact that Thor was a prisoner spoke against that. But Cecil needed to get Thor out of there, and he wouldn't be able to do it from where he was right now. He needed help. He needed Tryg and his powers.

Cecil didn't know where Tryg was, but he knew Tryg would come as soon as Cecil told him what was happening. They needed to be quick, before Fabrice did whatever he was planning to do.

There would be no coming back if he did.

CHAPTER SEVENTEEN

Thor wasn't sure whether he should be grateful to Fabrice or not. He was very much aware of the fact that the only reason Fabrice wanted to keep him there was torture him and Cecil. But no matter what his intentions were, it was better than having to face the conclave.

Thor had never been in front of them, but he'd heard of plenty of people who had. None of them had come back alive. The heroes were humans, or at least, they used to be human. They were enhanced when they became heroes. From Thor's point of view, their new powers and abilities, and their immortality, made them more similar to him and the other paranormal creatures than to humans, but no one had asked his opinion. It sounded a bit hypocritical, though. Heroes had been created to rid the world of paranormal creatures, yet in some ways, they'd become one of them.

None of that mattered right now, though. Thor didn't know what he was going to do. He allowed the hero to drag him toward the room Fabrice had decided he should be put in. He knew Fabrice would strike as soon as the hero was sleeping. Fabrice didn't seem to have realized what he was in for when he'd contacted the conclave, but now he did. He wouldn't give the hero a chance to take Thor away, not before he used him to get to his brother.

And Thor was alone.

He should have contacted Tryg at the very least, but he'd thought this was going to be easy. It should have been. It *would* have been if Fabrice hadn't realized what Thor was.

He'd known Thor would come eventually, and he'd made sure to be prepared when that happened. Now Thor was in trouble, and he had no way to get out of it.

He should be able to dream-walk if Fabrice and the hero gave him some time alone, but he couldn't count on that happening. It would be too easy, and they both knew what he could do. There was no way they would allow him to get free.

When they stepped into the room, the hero dragged Thor toward the wall. Thor arched a brow when he noticed the chains hanging from it. "Is this your torture room?" he asked Fabrice.

The hero frowned, but Fabrice was quick to answer. "Of course not. As you might know, this house belonged to my ancestors. Some of them were overeager when it came to punishing people, and this room is what's left of that. I've never personally used it, not in the sense you're implying."

Thor would have called bullshit, but he didn't think it was wise right now. The hero slammed Thor's back against the wall and wrapped his hand around his throat. Thor did his best not to look like he was having troubles breathing, but he doubted the hero cared. The man reached into his pocket and took out a small vial. Thor tried to push back, knowing he shouldn't drink it but also that he would, willing or not. Whatever was inside, it wouldn't be good for him.

The hero pushed his thumb against Thor's jaw. Thor gritted his teeth, but a well-placed knee to his groin made him gasp in pain, and the hero took that opportunity to stick the open vial into Thor's mouth. The liquid was bitter, and Thor spluttered, but the hero pushed his jaw up to make sure Thor didn't spit it out. He leaned closer. "This is going to make sure that you can't turn to smoke, or to any of the other animals you can become," he murmured.

The hero let go and turned toward Fabrice. "Thank you for offering me food and a place to rest. I won't sleep for long, but

I do need to before we leave."

The man really wasn't smart, was he? There was no way Fabrice wasn't going to try to kill Thor when the guy left, and the only reason he might not was that he wanted Cecil to see it and feel the pain. Or possibly, the other way around. Thor knew he'd angered Fabrice, and that Fabrice wanted to get revenge against him. Of course, the easiest way for that to happen would be to let the hero take him to the conclave. No paranormal creature had ever come back alive, and that was exactly what Fabrice wanted for him.

Fabrice smiled, and he was handsome enough that Thor could understand why the hero was eating out of his hand. "Of course. I'll get you something to eat from the kitchen. You can wait for me in the office."

Thor expected both to leave, and they did, but only a few minutes later, the door opened again. Thor strained against the chains that held him to the wall, but they didn't budge. The hero stepped into the room again and closed the door behind himself. He leaned against it, watching Thor.

"What?" Thor asked. Now wasn't the time to be a smart ass, no matter how hard it was to resist the urge.

"What did you do to him?"

"To Fabrice?"

The hero nodded. "Why does he want to see you dead so badly?"

"Why do you?"

"Because you're a creature. You have no place on earth."

Thor snorted. "That didn't sound rehearsed. Is that what they tell you at the conclave?"

The hero crossed his arms over his chest. "But you *are* a creature."

"Yes, I am. But so are you. You have to realize you're not human anymore."

Most heroes would have been offended to be called a

creature, especially when a hero's life was dedicated to killing what they saw as parasites. But not this guy. No, the only reaction Thor got out of him was a frown and, "I suppose I'm not. That doesn't make me an evil creature."

"The fact that I am a draugr doesn't make me one, either. I didn't choose to become this. And I don't even know how it happened, even after all those years. I did the best with what I had."

"You killed people."

"How do you know that? You know who I am? Did you before Fabrice contacted you?"

"All creatures like you kill people."

"Is that what they teach you at the conclave?" The hero stared until Thor decided to give him what he wanted. "Yes, I killed people. So did you."

"I killed monsters. That's what we do."

"That's what I do, too. I kill the people that human justice doesn't go after or can't go after. I kill people who have too much money and power for anyone to stop them. I kill people who treat other human beings as slaves, who traffic them and hurt them. Who do you kill? Innocent people? People whose only fault is not to be human? Because let me tell you, I doubt that most of your people check twice before deciding a creature should die."

Thor wasn't without fault. He'd killed a lot of monsters, but in his long life, he'd also killed people who hadn't deserved it. Still, he didn't want the hero to hide behind the righteousness the conclave liked so much. It was true that they sometimes got their hands on the right people, on creatures who took pleasure in torturing people. Yet now, the hero was in the house of one of them, and instead of taking care of Fabrice, he was going to take Thor away and hand him over to the conclave. How was that fair? Thor had done his best to keep humanity safe. He'd given back what he'd taken from it. Fabrice, on the other hand, didn't think twice about killing people to take their powers. How was Thor or anyone else supposed to believe in the conclave and what they did when they went after the wrong people? Or at least, when they went after *some* of the wrong people?

Because even if someone decided Thor should pay for what he'd done in the past, he shouldn't be the only one to pay. Fabrice was as bad as he'd ever been, if not more. Thor never enjoyed killing people. Fabrice did, and enormously so. He was keeping Thor there to torture his brother until Cecil gave him what he wanted.

"We only kill the creatures that deserve it," the hero said.

Thor snorted. "Right. Keep telling yourself that."

"The conclave gives us our orders. They know what they're doing."

"Sure they do. That's why they haven't told you about Fabrice, right?"

"What do you mean?"

"You should probably do a little research instead of accepting jobs without even thinking. Fabrice has been tearing through the paranormal communities all around the world for decades. He's been torturing people to steal their powers. But of course, you don't care about that, do you? They weren't human. There were creatures like me, not human anymore, maybe not ever. Why would you care, right?"

Thor hoped he was getting to the hero, but he had no way to know. This was his only option, though. He was alone, and that meant he had to find a way out of this on his own.

Cecil didn't know what he would have done without Tryg. He wouldn't have been able to get there as fast as they had, that was for sure. He didn't even care that it felt weird to be smoke with Tryg rather than Thor. The only thing he cared about was to sneak inside the house and get to Thor before something happened to him.

He hoped they were in time. They'd had to travel, and it had taken them time. It was less time than it would've taken Cecil to do this alone, but still. It had been more than long enough for Fabrice to hurt Thor. Cecil couldn't focus on that, though. He couldn't allow himself to be weak, not when he needed to be strong for Thor.

Tryg lowered them toward one of the open windows. Isaac had traveled with them, but Tryg had decided to leave him outside the property. He didn't want to put Isaac in danger, even though he was immortal, and that more than anything told Cecil he'd done the right thing when he'd manipulated Isaac's death. His new immortality wouldn't be used for bad things, only for love.

That didn't mean Isaac wouldn't have a hand in rescuing Thor. Cecil had found out that Isaac had been training with Tryg. He wasn't a hacker by any means, but he knew enough to keep an eye on satellite images of the house. He'd be able to tell them if someone came in or left. That was all they needed, at least for now.

Cecil didn't think there was anyone else in the house except for Fabrice, the hero, and Thor. Fabrice liked to do his thing alone, because that way he didn't have to answer to anyone or explain himself.

He's going to be expecting us, Tryg said in Cecil's mind.

That was even weirder than traveling in smoke form with him. *I know.* That was why he had no intention of rushing to Thor's side, even though he yearned to. Fabrice would know that was what he wanted to do, and he'd make sure to get to Cecil before it happened.

There was also the hero to think about. Tryg had said he'd be the one to take care of the man, but Cecil wasn't going to abandon him to it, not when neither of them was sure he could beat the hero. Cecil had no experience fighting heroes, but just like every single person in the paranormal community, he knew about them. They were strong, and there weren't human. It was almost impossible to kill them. It wasn't his and Tryg's first objective, but they both knew they'd have to face the guy.

Cecil wasn't sure what frightened him most—the hero or his brother.

Tryg didn't hesitate as he floated them through an open window. He was the one in charge, and Cecil was more than happy to let him. Cecil was just along for the ride, although hopefully, tonight was the night when he'd finally be able to be free of his brother. He didn't care how that happened, but he suspected he would have to be the one to do it. He wasn't looking forward to it, mostly because he knew Fabrice was stronger than him, but he'd do what he had to do. Either way, he'd be free tonight.

Where is he exactly? Tryg asked.

I don't know. He was in the office, but I think Fabrice decided to move him. It would make sense, and Fabrice was smart enough to know that. *My brother knows that Thor is a draugr, so he'll expect someone to come to help him as smoke.*

Let me worry about that. Focus on Thor and on finding him.

There's an old cell downstairs.

A cell?

Yes. This house is ancient, and they used to keep prisoners here. It wasn't a surprise that the place was one of Fabrice's favorite. It probably appealed to his inner serial killer.

Guide me to the cell.

It took them a few tries, because he didn't remember a lot of details about the time he'd spent there. Fabrice had locked him in the cell the only time he'd been in the house, and it wasn't something Cecil wanted to think about or remember. Fabrice had hated Cecil even before their mother had died, and only her intervention had gotten Cecil freed back then.

But they found the cell, and the doors were open. Cecil's chest felt like it was frozen and like he'd never breathe again, but he pushed through the feeling as they went into the room.

Thor was chained to the wall. Cecil had expected it, but the sight still made his heart feel like it stopped. Instead of focusing on Thor like he wanted to, he forced himself to look at the other two people in the room. Fabrice and the hero were facing each other, and they both looked angry. Fabrice was gesturing, but the hero didn't look like he would change his mind, whatever Fabrice said.

"I called you. You wouldn't have him if it wasn't for me."

The hero didn't miss a beat. "And the conclave is grateful for that. It doesn't mean we'll allow you to torture him."

"But you're going to do it anyway, aren't you? What difference does it make, if the conclave does it or if I do?"

"We're not going to torture him. He has to die, but it doesn't have to be done cruelly."

Fabrice didn't get the opportunity to push because Tryg chose that moment to turn him and Cecil back to their human form. They'd discussed this, so Cecil made a beeline for his brother, ignoring the hero and Thor. He stood in front of Fabrice, ready to die or to kill — or do both.

Fabrice's smile was wicked. "I knew you'd come."

"And here I am."

"You were always the stupid one. You know what I'm going to do to you, right? You shouldn't have come. You were always too soft-hearted. That's why you shouldn't have been given our mother's power."

Cecil was done discussing things. He'd tried when he'd been in Fabrice's mind, and he wouldn't get different results. He wasn't going to try again. There was no way to save his brother, and he had to focus on saving himself.

He wasn't sure how he was going to do that, though.

He didn't know where to start. As a half hag, he had some

control over nature. His mother had taught him how to do some things while Fabrice had always refused even to try. Fabrice thought those powers were weak, and maybe he was right. That wasn't going to stop Cecil.

The cell was empty but for the chains on the wall, but there was a small window up high on the wall. Cecil knew that the cell was in the basement, and that meant roots. He reached out with his power and found them. He pulled, making them grow. They pushed through the wall, stone and mortar crumbling to the floor. His brother escaped one of the roots reaching for him, but another two wrapped around his arm and leg.

Instead of freaking out, Fabrice laughed.

His hands caught fire, and the roots disappeared in smoke. Cecil tried to use another root to block Fabrice, but Fabrice was faster, and he managed to burn them before they even touched him.

Then he turned his attention to Cecil.

He hurled a fireball at Cecil's head. Cecil ducked, but the smell told him part of his hair was gone. His hair was the last thing he cared about right now, though. He rolled on the floor, away from Fabrice. He needed to regroup, but his lack of training when it came to fighting was hindering him.

Roots weren't the only thing that was in the earth beyond the walls. While still working to avoid Fabrice's fireballs, Cecil pulled on the moisture in the earth. There wasn't a lot of it, but it was enough to snuff out the fires on his brother's hands.

Cecil took advantage of Fabrice's surprise to wrap a root around his waist.

What now?

Cecil didn't want to think about killing his brother, but it was the only way out. He pulled onto one of the roots and molded it into a point. He hesitated, and that brief moment was enough for Fabrice to burn the root around his waist and reach for Cecil.

Cecil's skin burned. It hurt but allowing his brother to torture him would hurt more. Fabrice couldn't kill him, not when he needed Cecil to give over their mother's power. But Cecil wasn't the only one with the power to control the roots. Fabrice might not be trained in it, but he could use it, and he pinned Cecil against the wall.

Cecil quickly killed the roots around his arms with his power to manipulate death and dropped to his feet. To his surprise, he punched Fabrice right on the nose. Fabrice staggered back, his eyes wide and his nose bleeding. Cecil got another punch in before Fabrice reacted.

Fabrice moved his hands in a complicated gesture, and something invisible pushed at Cecil's chest. Cecil fell, and he was slammed to the floor, air whooshing out of his lungs with the force of the impact.

Fabrice stood over him, sneering, his face red with blood. "You're going to pay for that."

Cecil tried to suck in a breath, but it was like the surrounding air was gone. He croaked, trying to talk, but no words came out of his mouth.

Fabrice's smile widened. He looked like a madman, but Cecil knew he wasn't. "I'm going to torture you. I'm going to hurt your draugr, and I'm going to force you to watch and hear his every scream. But I won't kill him. No, I'll keep him alive and hurt him until you give me your power. Then I'll start on you. He's going to have to hear you scream, too."

Cecil needed to get out of this, but he couldn't. He couldn't even breathe. The corners of the room were becoming black in his vision, and Cecil knew he didn't have long before he fainted. He tried to move, but he was pinned to the ground, his brother controlling the air pressure.

Fabrice opened his mouth, but this time, instead of words coming out, blood did. A sword stuck out of his chest, right next to his heart.

Fabrice looked down, his eyes wide as if he couldn't quite believe what was happening.

Cecil understood the feeling. He couldn't quite believe it either. More blood dripped from Fabrice's mouth. He reached for the sword, but he couldn't do anything about it. The press on Cecil's chest lessened, then entirely disappeared, and Cecil watched as his brother fell to his knees, then to his side.

Then died.

Thor needed someone to take him down. He pulled on the chains, but they didn't move, just like Fabrice had intended them to. He'd wanted Thor to watch while he hurt Cecil, and that had almost happened. It *had* happened, and Thor needed to get to Cecil.

The scene in front of him was staggering in so many ways. It felt like he and Cecil had been running from Fabrice for weeks, even though it had been nowhere that long. Now Fabrice was lying on the floor, dead, and he was dead because the hero had killed him.

They were lucky Fabrice wasn't a draugr. A sword in the chest wouldn't have killed him then, and Cecil would have been hurt more than he was now.

And why was Cecil still on the floor?

For fuck's sake. Thor jerked the chains forward, and while he felt them give it a bit, it wasn't nearly enough for him to free himself. He got Tryg's attention, but Tryg didn't move from his spot by the hero. He was ready to act if the man made one move toward Thor or Cecil. That was good, but it would be better if Thor was free and could do something, too. He could see Cecil was bleeding, and the fact that he was moving wasn't as reassuring as it should have been.

"Cecil? Can you hear me?" Thor yelled. It broke the silence

in the room, and everyone started to move at once.

Cecil groaned and tried to stand, but he staggered even before he could get to his feet. Thor tried once again to pull away from the wall, and this time, Tryg stepped toward him. Thor wasn't sure how he felt about Tryg leaving the hero alone. The hero had killed Fabrice, but that didn't mean he was done for the day. He was there to get Thor back to his conclave, and usually, heroes did exactly what they were told. They didn't think. They didn't wonder if the people they were killing deserved it. This one seemed different, but Thor couldn't put any trust in appearances, not when Cecil's life might be in danger.

Thor kept an eye on the hero while Tryg worked on the chains. He was surprised when the hero didn't move, not even to get his sword back from Fabrice's chest. It had been a good shot. Thor hadn't seen what had happened, because he'd been focused on Fabrice and Cecil, and he was curious, but not so much that most of his attention wasn't on Cecil.

Tryg finally freed one of Thor's wrists, then the other. Thor's entire body hurt because of the stretched position he'd been in for so long, and he had to rub his wrists to get feeling back into them. The skin there was red and raw, and it hurt. It was relatively easy to ignore the pain when he rushed to Cecil's side, though. He kneeled next to Cecil and pushed him back down when Cecil tried to get up again.

"Are you okay?" Thor asked. It was probably a stupid question, but he needed to ask it, and he needed an answer to it.

"I've been better." Cecil tried to smile, but it looked more like a grimace than a smile. "Is he dead?"

Thor didn't have to ask him who he was talking about. "He's dead," he confirmed.

Cecil's shoulders slumped in what Thor hoped was relief rather than pain. "Good."

"Oh no, you don't," Tryg growled from behind them.

Thor jumped to his feet and turned to face the hero. Cecil was safe for the first time in decades. Thor wasn't going to let anyone change that. But the hero looked harmless. Of course, that could be because he was a gorgeous blond, but Thor had learned to look past appearances a long time ago. The hero had raised both hands in what looked like a placating gesture. He wasn't moving toward Cecil and Thor anymore, so that was good, but he did look like he was about to do something. Thor didn't know what, but he wanted to find out. The hero's behavior was weird enough that Thor wanted answers from him.

"I wasn't going to hurt anyone," the hero said.

"And we're supposed to believe that?" Tryg asked.

"My brother made you come here to kill Thor." Cecil sounded pissed, even though he was still on the floor.

The hero nodded curtly. "He did."

"So you're going to try to do it."

"That *is* why I was here originally. But I see that the situation was nothing like Fabrice told me and the conclave."

Cecil snorted. "That's Fabrice for you." His expression turned more serious. "Why did you kill him?"

"Because he was a monster. The things he said to you . . ."

"He would have done every single one of them."

"I realized that while he was talking."

Cecil gently pushed against Thor's shoulder. It got Thor's attention, and Thor scowled at him when he realized Cecil was still trying to get up. Cecil ignored him, of course, and Thor knew better than to tell him to sit back down. When Cecil wanted to do something, he did it, even if it was a stupid idea. At least this time, Thor would be there to catch him if he fell.

Cecil was fairly steady on his feet, so Thor felt okay taking a step back. He didn't go far, though. He wouldn't give the hero a chance to hurt Cecil. He didn't like it when Cecil stepped closer to the hero, but he'd already known that was what Cecil was planning to do.

What he hadn't expected was for Cecil to hold his hand out to the hero. From the look of things, neither had Tryg and the hero.

The hero looked down at the hand, blinking.

Cecil gave him the time he needed to realize what was happening—which Thor thought was way too long considering the guy was supposed to be the protector of humanity or some shit like that—without pushing or saying anything. Thor tensed when the hero took Cecil's hand, but nothing other than a handshake happened.

"Thank you," Cecil said.

To Thor's surprise, the hero's cheeks reddened. "I was doing my job."

"We're going to have to agree to disagree on this one. Your job was to take Thor back to the conclave. Instead, you killed my brother."

"My job is to get rid of the evil and monsters that populate the earth. That's what I did."

Thor was *not* going to snort.

"I'm Cecil."

The hero looked nonplussed, but he answered, "I'm Haven."

Of course he had a ridiculously blond name.

Cecil smiled. "And you already know Tryg and Thor."

The hero spared them a glance. "I do."

"They're not bad people. I'm not saying they've never done anything bad in their long life, but they've been working to help humanity for decades. Humans need them, even though they don't know they do. I don't want to hurt you, and I don't think they want to either, but we will if you try to take them to your conclave."

Cecil surprised everyone once again when he placed himself in between Haven and Tryg and Thor. He had to be exhausted and in pain, but he didn't look like it when he spread his arms out and roots shot from the walls. Thor had been stunned when it had first happened while Cecil had been fighting Fabrice. For some reason, he and Cecil hadn't talked about what Cecil could do beyond his power of manipulating death. But he seemed to have a lot of secrets up his sleeves, and that was okay. Thor couldn't wait to spend the rest of their lives discovering them.

The roots stopped before touching Haven, but from the way they twitched, it was obvious they were ready to strike as soon as Haven did something Cecil didn't like. The four of them stared at each other, and Thor knew they were all holding their breath. He didn't care much about Cecil hurting Haven—he didn't care about Cecil hurting any hero, to be honest—but Cecil was tired and wounded. Thor didn't want him to use his powers again.

But even though he needed food and a bed, Cecil was standing up for Thor. He was standing up for him, and he looked ready to tear Haven's head off his shoulders if he made even one move to hurt Thor. The only other person who'd ever done something like that was Tryg, and Thor wasn't quite sure what to do with the warmth that filled his chest.

"You're protecting them," Haven said.

Cecil thought his name didn't fit him. He was so big, and he looked like a warrior, yet his name was one of peace, one that soothed people rather than killed them. "I am."

"Why?"

That was easy to answer. "Because they're good men. They didn't have to help me when they realized my brother was trying to kill me, yet they did. They didn't have to help Isaac when they discovered him chained to a man's wall, yet they did. Even after helping him, they could have left him somewhere alone because he wasn't their problem, but Tryg is still with him. And I know Thor is going to stick with me until I'm ready to be on my own. And it's not only me. They've been killing the human monsters your people don't care about."

Haven's shoulders tensed. "I never said we didn't care about the human monsters."

"Maybe not, but you're also not doing anything to get rid of them. Thor and Tryg are. Look, what you do or don't do has nothing to do with the situation. You think Tryg and Thor are monsters because of what they are, and you don't take into consideration what they do. I could say the same about you."

Haven jerked back as if Cecil had slapped him. "I'm not a monster."

"I don't think you are, but you're not human, are you?"

"Not anymore."

At least he was ready to admit that. Cecil wasn't sure what he would have done otherwise. "You're in the same boat as Tryg and Thor, then. They were human once, and they're not anymore. It wasn't their choice, but they've done their best with what life gave them. What do you think they should have done? Kill themselves as soon as they woke up as draugr? Why are your people better just because you're a different kind of paranormal creature? Who decided that?"

Haven raised his hands. "I get it. You don't have to explain. I wasn't going to hurt either of them, and I realized that Fabrice was the one who I should have dealt with from the beginning."

Cecil wanted to ask why Haven had been sent to kill Thor rather than his brother, but he didn't care. As long as Thor and Tryg were safe and were allowed to leave this place, he didn't care about anything else.

"Are you going to come after them in the future?" Cecil asked.

"I don't know. I'm not the one who makes that kind of decision."

"Your conclave does."

"They do. I don't know why Fabrice wasn't on their radar, but I'm going to find out. That's all I can promise."

That was all Cecil wanted right now. He dropped his hands and along with them, the control he had over the roots. He staggered, more tired than he'd initially thought he was. But Thor was there, wrapping his arm around Cecil's waist and pulling him against his chest. Cecil snuggled against him, relieved and happy. He hadn't thought this was going to end the way it had. He hadn't thought he'd still be standing at the end of it. But he was. Both he and Thor were. Cecil had no idea what that meant for the future, but at least they'd have a chance to find out.

Haven raked a hand through his hair. "You'd better leave."

Cecil looked at his brother's body. He wasn't sure what to do about it. He didn't like leaving Fabrice there, but he didn't have the time or the inclination to do anything about it. Fabrice hadn't been his brother in too long. This wasn't Cecil's job anymore, and Cecil didn't feel guilty as he turned away from Fabrice. "Why?"

"Because another two heroes were supposed to arrive today to help me get Thor to the conclave. I called them since Fabrice didn't want to let me leave with Thor."

"Why are you letting us go?" It couldn't be that easy, could it? Not that today had been easy, but the situation with Haven *was* easier than Cecil had thought it would be. He'd expected to have to fight, but instead, Haven was giving in without asking questions.

"I am. It's obvious to me that Fabrice was the bad guy in

this situation. He's not who I was supposed to kill, but killing him was the right thing to do."

"How do we know you're not going to come after us?" Tryg asked.

"You don't, not for sure. You'll have to trust me on this and believe me. I realize how weird that is. But you don't have a choice here, and neither do I."

"What will happen to you if you don't bring Thor to the conclave?" Cecil asked. He didn't want Haven to get hurt, but he wasn't sure there was anything he could do about it, not beyond giving Thor up, and that wasn't something he was ready to do.

"Nothing. This isn't the first time I've failed to do a job."

"That means they're going to send you after Thor again?" As long as it wasn't tomorrow or the day after that, it didn't matter. Cecil wasn't going anywhere, not for the long run, and he'd make sure Thor was protected.

"Possibly. They won't be happy that I failed to get him, and I *am* going to have to find him again if he hurts someone he shouldn't. But for the moment, he should be safe. The three of you should be."

Cecil bit his lower lip. He was sure Haven wasn't telling them everything. They weren't friends. They weren't even allies beyond this moment. But he couldn't brush off the feeling that something bad was going to happen to Haven once he got back to the conclave. Even if the conclave didn't punish him for not doing his job, it was obvious the heroes weren't as good as everyone thought—including themselves, or rather, *especially* themselves. Cecil hadn't had many interactions with heroes, but like everyone else in their world, he knew who they were and what they did.

They were humans who'd been born with a mark that differentiated them from the rest of the people on earth. They'd been offered the chance to keep humanity safe. They'd stopped being human to do that. Some of them were self-righteous about it. They liked to flaunt their sacrifices, and they didn't think twice about killing the people they considered monsters because they'd been chosen to do that, so they had to be right, didn't they? Thor and Tryg were lucky that Haven seemed to be different. Haven's diversity worried Cecil, though. He wanted Haven to know he wasn't alone in the world, that if he needed help against the conclave for whatever reason, he'd have it.

They weren't friends, but that didn't mean they couldn't *become* friends. Cecil didn't expect it to be easy by any means considering the history between Haven, Thor, and Tryg, but that wouldn't stop him.

He detangled himself from Thor and stepped closer to Haven. "Do you have a cell phone?" he asked.

Haven frowned. "Of course I have a cell phone."

"Okay. Take it out. I'm going to give you my phone number. I want you to call me if you need help, for anything."

"Cecil!" Thor snapped.

Cecil ignored him. He gave his number to Haven once Haven finally got his phone out of his pocket. "I meant it. It's obvious that something is wrong with the conclave and how they make their decisions, and that you'll investigate this. I just want you to know that you're not alone. You could have killed the three of us without thinking twice about it, but instead, you're letting us go, potentially putting yourself at risk. I won't forget that. I owe you."

Haven shook his head. "You don't owe me anything. You were right. Your brother was the one who deserved to die today, not Thor. And you're right that I'll investigate what's up with the conclave."

"Use my number if you ever need to, please. Even if you don't think I owe you anything. Everyone deserves to have support, and that includes you. Just like you can't say all paranormal creatures are monsters, not all heroes blindly follow the conclave, and we both know that's going to become a problem for you."

Cecil didn't have anything else to say. He turned around, ignored Thor's rolling eyes, and pressed himself against him. He sighed in relief and closed his eyes, knowing when they became smoke even without looking around by the feeling of Thor and Tryg in his mind.

They were going home.

EPILOGUE

Thor was lonely. He wasn't sure when that had happened. He was used to being on his own, after all. He'd been on his own for hundreds of years, with only an occasional visit from Tryg and his other few friends. But now, Cecil was gone, and Thor felt *lonely*. It wasn't a feeling he was used to, and he didn't like it. That was why he was planning to do something about it.

He and Cecil had spent a few days together after Fabrice had been killed. They both needed to heal and to rest. They'd gone back to the cottage while Tryg and Isaac went to one of Tryg's caves. Thor still wasn't sure what Tryg's fascination with caves was, even though they shared the same sensitivity to light. All that stone had to be fucking cold.

But once Cecil had healed, he'd told Thor he had things to do. Thor understood it. Cecil had stopped living for so long while his brother hunted him, and now his brother's death had put it back in motion. Cecil needed to put his life in order, especially with the way he'd had to leave it behind in Brussels. He'd wanted to fix the apartment and to talk to the landlord.

As far as Thor knew, Cecil was there now. They'd texted, but Thor hadn't wanted to be overwhelming. Neither he nor Cecil was used to being in a relationship. Thor wasn't sure how to go about it, and he didn't want to be overbearing. Cecil deserved time on his own to figure out what was next for him.

Even if that didn't include Thor.

Thor wasn't sure how he'd deal with it if that was the case, but he wouldn't worry about it until — unless — it happened.

Which was why he was now standing in front of Cecil's door in Brussels. He had no idea what was going to happen when he'd knock. Cecil might be happy to see him, or he might not be, and this would be a disaster. Either way, Thor had to know. He needed to be sure before he got himself in too deep to step back.

They should have talked about the future when they'd had the opportunity. They'd both avoided it, though. Thor suspected it had been for the same reason — they were both afraid of what the other might say, of rejection. Neither of them had wanted to risk it, and now here they were, separated by only a door, and they'd never felt so far apart.

Thor raised his hand to knock, but before his fist could hit the door, a yell made him freeze.

"How could you?"

That was Cecil. Thor would have recognized his voice anywhere. He had no clue who was in the apartment with him, though, and that meant he didn't know if he should intervene or not.

"I didn't have a choice," a woman answered.

"You could have come to me. You *should* have come to me. I don't understand why you didn't."

"He was going to *kill* me, Cecil. What would you have done in my place?"

"I would have fucking talked to me. You should know that you can always do that. I would have done everything I could to help you. You're my best friend. You *were* my best friend."

The woman sobbed. This was a serious conversation, and Thor wondered if he should step away and leave Cecil and the woman to it. Whatever he and Cecil had to tell each other, it could wait. Besides, Thor doubted Cecil was going to be in the mood for their conversation once his fight with the woman was over.

"Leave," Cecil said. His voice was icy and calm, and it was like a dagger to the heart. Thor could too easily imagine how the woman felt. It sounded like she and Cecil had been friends, and the way he was talking to her right now had to hurt, no matter how warranted it was.

"Cecil, please. You have to see —"

"The only thing I see right now is that you betrayed me, Mabel. I can't look at you anymore. Leave, please."

Thor had to take a step back when the door slammed open so it wouldn't hit his face. A woman ran past him, and he watched her go. He didn't know whether he should go inside the apartment. He wanted to comfort Cecil, but would it be welcome?

"Thor?"

Cecil didn't sound as strong and calm as he had only seconds ago. His voice trembled, and his eyes were filling with tears. Thor didn't think twice about it. He walked into the apartment and opened his arms, and Cecil stepped into them.

He clung to Thor's t-shirt, his shoulders trembling as he sobbed. Thor wanted to shield him from the world and the pain he was feeling, but there was nothing he could do but hold him. So that was what he did.

They stood there for a long time, wrapped around each other with the door open. No one came by, luckily, and Thor was able to focus on Cecil. He rubbed his hands on Cecil's back and murmured whatever soothing words he could think of. He had even less experience with comforting people than he had with relationships, but if he wanted this to work, he'd need to get used to it. Cecil was a touchy-feely kind of person, and unlike to Thor, he didn't have a problem talking about his feelings. It would take a while to work on that, but Thor could do it.

Once the worst seemed to have passed, Thor guided Cecil toward the couch. The apartment looked like it had the last time Thor had been there, comfortable and cozy. He settled Cecil on the couch and went to close the door, then made his way to the kitchen to get a glass of water. Cecil was drying his eyes when Thor got back to him, and he took the glass with a wobbly smile.

"I don't know what you're doing here, but you're a sight for sore eyes," he said after sipping half the glass.

"I wanted to see you. I hope it's okay."

Cecil patted the couch next to him. He didn't have to ask for Thor to sit down, and once Thor was there, he wrapped Cecil into his arms again. Cecil came easily, settling against Thor's chest as if he belonged there. Thor hoped he did.

"Do you want to talk about it?" he asked.

Cecil sighed heavily. "That was Mabel, my best friend, or at least I thought she was. I just found out she was the one who told Fabrice we were in Scotland."

Thor wasn't sure what to say about that. He wanted to rage against her because she'd put Cecil's life in danger, but he didn't want to badmouth her in front of Cecil. He didn't know if Cecil would ever be able to forgive her for what she'd done, but just in case, he didn't want to make things worse.

"I can't believe she did that," Cecil said.

"From what I heard, he threatened her."

"I know. I'm not surprised he did. It's Fabrice we're talking about. But I don't know if I can ever trust her again. She was the only person in the world I trusted before I met you. She should have come to me and talked about this instead of doing what Fabrice wanted her to do. He's taking things away from me even now that he's dead."

Thor kissed Cecil's hair. "He won't take me away from you."

Cecil tilted his head to look at Thor. "That's why you're here? To show me you're still with me?"

"Pretty much. We should have talked before you left. I

spent the past few weeks obsessing over what was going on between us and wondering if we have a future. I decided it was time to stop wondering and get answers."

Cecil wrapped his arms around Thor's neck. "My answer is yes."

Thor's heart skipped a beat even though he hadn't asked Cecil to marry him—yet. "Yes?"

"I want to be with you. I've been thinking about it ever since I left, too, and I've been wondering why I decided that coming here without you was a good idea in the first place. I shouldn't have."

"You needed time to yourself. I understand that."

"I did, but I shouldn't have ignored you the way I did. I guess I was afraid that you were going to take this opportunity to distance yourself from me, so I did it instead of waiting for you to. I wasn't sure I could face that, not yet."

"You don't have to. I'm not going anywhere."

"Yeah?" Cecil asked with a smile.

"Yeah. I don't know how things will go, but I do know that you're it for me. It sounds ridiculous, but it's true. I want to spend the rest of my life with you, or at least a few hundred years. We can start from there and see what happens next."

Cecil laughed, and Thor knew he'd made the right decision. He was done surviving. It was time to start living—for both of them.

You may also enjoy the following from eXtasy Books Inc:

Ulric
Catherine Lievens

Excerpt

Ulric pushed the scientist to his knees. The man stumbled as he fell, but Ulric didn't attempt to keep him upright. None of the people he and the others had caught tonight deserved that kind of regard. They were monsters, plain and simple, even though there were human.

Ulric had expected what he'd found in the cells and the operating rooms. He'd been through this once already, and that time, he'd been one of those who got rescued. He wasn't this time, and he was glad he could help these people. No one deserved to be locked in a cell. No one deserved to be turned into something they were never meant to be. Ulric was lucky enough he'd gotten used to his new ability. All the assassins had, and thanks to those abilities, they'd found a job and a makeshift family. Not everyone would be so lucky, though.

And not everyone was made to be an assassin.

Killing people, even though they deserved it, was hard. What Ulric and the other assassins did was done in cold blood. They didn't act under the fire of emotions, and they didn't have regrets. Ulric had learned a long time ago not to have them. The people he and the other killed didn't deserve to be thought about twice once they were dead. They hurt and killed vulnerable people, children, and death was the only thing they deserved.

"Is that it?" Roark asked.

They'd gathered everyone in the closest room big enough by the elevators. There were going to need easy access once they started getting people out of there, but none of them wanted the prisoners to see the people who had tortured them while they finally walked toward freedom and safety. Once all of them were out and in healers' hands, the enforcers would get the scientists and guards away and shimmer them to the council jail. They would have done that already, but of course, the entire floor was shielded to Nix.

Cora nodded. "I asked a few enforcers to do one last check on this house, but I think we got all the bad guys out."

"The prisoners?"

"We left them in the cells as you ordered."

It had been hard. Ulric had walked into a few cells to try to reassure the prisoners, and he'd wanted to take those people to freedom, but it was safer for them to stay where they were while the enforcer and the assassins take care of their jailers. Now that the bad guys were locked up, they were going to be able to free the prisoners, and Ulric couldn't wait. He still remembered how it felt, and he wanted to give that to someone else, to reassure them and show them they could make it, that they didn't have to be what the scientists and the people paying them had planned for them to be.

Lawrence appeared at the door. He was alone, but then, all the bad guys were already in the room. He saw Roark and made a beeline for him. "We have a problem."

Roark frowned. "A problem?"

"One of the prisoners. I went into this room, and the scientists were forcing him to try to set up a bunny on fire, I think. I tried talking to him, and I don't know what the scientists did to him, but he's on fire."

Roark's eyes widened. "We need to evacuate."

Lawrence shook his head. "That's not why I'm here. Sky is in a fireproof room. Everyone here is safe, I promise. But the problem is that Sky can't turn the fire off. From what I understand, his ability to catch fire is linked to his emotions. When he feels strongly, poof."

Ulric blinked. "Poof?"

Lawrence shrugged. "Pretty much. I have no idea how it happened or what was done to him, but since Cora can control fire, I thought she might be able to help him."

Roark nodded. "All right. You take Cora and go to him, maybe Tony too since his ability with ice and cold could be useful. The rest of us will get everyone out. We'll let you know when it's safe to take him out of the fireproof room."

Ulric had to see this. Since Roark hadn't given him a direct order, he followed Lawrence, Cora, and Tony out of the room. They had to walk toward the back of the floor, and Ulric recognized it. He'd walked into a small room with two scientists watching something through a glass earlier. He'd knocked them out and had dragged them to the elevators, but he hadn't stopped to check through the glass because Lawrence had been there. He should have known better than to ignore it, and he hated himself for not trying to do something for this Sky guy. Not that he could have done much since fire wasn't his forte, but he could have tried to reassure Sky.

The guy was on fire. Lawrence had already explained this, but Ulric hadn't expected it to look like this. What looked like a man was curled up in the corner of the room, his knees against his chest. Ulric couldn't see much of Sky since he was on fire, but he looked on the smaller side, or maybe that was because he was sitting on the floor curled up into a ball.

A few enforcers had followed them into the room, but thankfully, they stayed by the door. Their eyes were wide, and Ulric knew he'd have looked very much like them he hadn't seen Cora deal with fire already. But he knew what she could do, and he suspected that Sky was like her. She was the best person to help him, so Ulric stayed at a distance. He was close enough to intervene if something went wrong, but not so close that Sky would freak out because of him. Tony stood next to him, his gaze fixed on Sky and Cora as she stepped closer. He was tense, ready to step in just like Ulric was.

"Hi. I'm Cora."

It was hard to say if Sky was looking at her. His face was turned toward her, so Ulric thought he was.

"You need to leave," Sky said.

"I'm not going anywhere. I can help you. I promise."

"You don't understand. I can't turn it off. I'm dangerous."

He shrunk against the wall when Cora moved even closer. She reached for him, and Ulric held his breath even though he knew nothing would happen to her. He heard the enforcers behind him cry out, but it was too late. Cora had taken Sky's hand, and nothing had happened to her. She didn't seem to be in pain because she wasn't. She could create fire and control it, and if she wanted, she could get her entire body to catch fire, just like Sky's. She was different from him because she had control over it, but that had come in time.

"How?" Sky asked. There was wonder in his voice, the same wonder Ulric felt watching them. No matter how used he was to Cora's ability, it was always incredible to watch her use it.

Cora smiled. "I told you I can help you. I was like you once. I learned control, and you can, too."

Sky snorted. "Not in time to get out of here. I'm ready to bet it's not something you learned in minutes."

"You're right, it's not. But we're not going to leave you here. I want to sedate you."

Sky tried to press harder against the wall, but there was nowhere for him to go. "I don't want to be sedated."

"I know that's what the scientists who did this to you did. I also know you don't know if you can trust us. I can make as many promises as I want, but it's not going to change that fact.

You'll have to trust me. I promise I'll teach you control as soon as you're out of here. But you have to get out of here first, and that won't happen if you're still on fire. I can help you calm down, but with everything happening, I doubt you'll manage. The only way out for you right now is to be sedated."

Ulric thought Sky was going to say no. He would have if he'd been in Sky's place. The last thing he would have wanted when he'd been freed from the lab was to be knocked out. Just thinking about it would have terrified him.

But Sky was stronger than him. He took a moment to think about it, then he nodded. "Promise you'll make sure I don't hurt anyone."

"Of course. But if your ability is anything like mine, you won't catch fire if you're not conscious."

"I've never woken up on fire."

"Then you won't this time, either."

Cora reached for her waist. She took out a syringe and held it up. "I'm going to need you to focus on putting the fire out in your arm. I know it's hard, but this is going to melt otherwise."

Ulric held his breath as Cora walked Sky through it. He was surprised that Sky managed, and soon after, he was asleep. Cora leaned back, and her shoulders relaxed. She turned toward Tony and Ulric. "I need one of you to carry him."

Ulric stepped forward. The enforcers did, too, but Ulric glared at them until they stepped back again. He reached Cora and crouched next to her. "I'll do it."

Cora looked as tired as Ulric self. "Thank you."

Ulric reached for Sky. Now that he could see the man, he couldn't help but notice how good he looked. He had long brown tangled hair, and while shorter than Ulric, it wasn't by much. He was too thin, which wasn't surprising considering he had to have been in the lab for a while. Ulric wouldn't have a hard time carrying him.

The smell hit him when he leaned over Sky. Sky smelled of

smoke, of something wild and untamable, and he smelled of Ulric's mate.

ABOUT THE AUTHOR

Catherine lives in Italy, country of good food and hot men. She used to write fantasy as a child, but it was reading her first gay erotic romance novel that made her realize that that was what she really wanted to write.

After graduating from college in English language and translation, she divides her day between writing, reading, taking care of her son and reading some more.

You can find her on Facebook and Twitter or on her web-site: authorcatherinelievens.wordpress.com

Email: lievens.catherine@gmail.com

Newsletter: http://eepurl.com/c-uvKn